Montana Cowboy Daddy

Montana Cowboy Daddy

A Wyatt Brothers Romance

Jane Porter

Montana Cowboy Daddy
Copyright© 2021 Jane Porter
Tule Publishing First Printing, April 2021

The Tule Publishing, Inc.

ALL RIGHTS RESERVED

First Publication by Tule Publishing 2021

Cover design by Lee Hyat at www.LeeHyat.com

No part of this book may be used or reproduced in any manner whatsoever without written permission except in the case of brief quotations embodied in critical articles and reviews.

This is a work of fiction. Names, characters, places, and incidents are products of the author's imagination or are used fictitiously. Any resemblance to actual events, locales, organizations, or persons, living or dead, is entirely coincidental.

ISBN: 978-1-954894-01-3

Dedication

For my Ty
My one and only…
The great love of my life.
There is you, and only you,
And you inspire every hero
in every story.
Love you this life and next.

Prologue

THE CALL CAME in the middle of the night, jolting Erika Baylor awake and then sending her dressing and grabbing her keys and purse to dash to her car.

She drove through the night to reach the Las Vegas police station, and during that long silent drive, her mind had raced, trying to grapple with everything that had happened. Her cousin April had been killed in a car accident. She'd left behind a baby. A baby Erika hadn't even known about.

Where was the baby's father?

Who was the baby's father?

Erika had never thought of herself as maternal. She wasn't one of those women that had grown up playing house, tucking in her dolls, and dreaming of being a mommy, not when her own mother had been sorely lacking in maternal love herself. But after arriving in Las Vegas and having social services place the soft bundle of a boy in her arms, explaining that April's mother wanted no part of the baby and had already suggested Beck Wyatt Estes be placed in foster care, Erika vowed to do right by Beck, which in her mind meant finding the infant's father, because maybe, just maybe, the father—whoever he was—would want his son.

She didn't think further than that. She wouldn't let herself think further than that as she was a full-time student, working on her dissertation for her doctorate in psychology, and she was stretched thin as it was, with little free time and next to no income. But an emergency was an emergency, and she took the baby, and April's personal effects, and promised to remain in town for the next few days while arrangements were made for her cousin's body and so forth.

Social services sent Erika off with a car seat and a diaper bag, along with April's purse, which contained her wallet, some pill bottles, and a set of keys. Erika had helped buckling the car seat into the back seat of her car, and tucked the crying baby into the car seat, and then using April's driver's license, set off for April's apartment, several miles off the Las Vegas Strip.

The baby was still wailing when Erika arrived at the complex and wailed as she lifted the car seat out and carried the baby, diaper bag, and purses upstairs. It took a number of tries before Erika got the right key in the right lock, but once she did, the door opened and she was in. Lights on, Erika's gaze swept the small unit. The apartment was a mess, the sink filled with dishes, the bedroom floor heaped with dirty laundry, the small dining table was heaped with clean laundry not yet folded.

She jiggled the crying baby as she opened the blinds and then opened the windows to air out the stale air, and then, while Beck continued fussing, she went through the cupboards looking for his normal formula and bottles. Social services had sent her home with a few cans in a makeshift diaper bag, but surely April had something here for him. But there wasn't much in the cupboards or the refrigerator. The tin of formula on the counter was empty and April, a dancer, seemed to have survived on fat-free yogurts, vodka, and cigarettes.

Troubled, Erika opened one of the cans of formula sent home with them, made a bottle, and sat down on the couch with Beck and let him drink his fill as she gazed around the apartment that clearly wasn't much of a home. From the bottles of Xanax and Ativan in April's purse, it was clear that she hadn't been doing well. Erika wondered how she'd coped alone for the past several months.

Suddenly Beck's hand reached up and his tiny fingers brushed hers. Erika glanced down and discovered he was staring straight up into her face, his dark blue eyes locking with hers. For the first time since she'd gotten the call about April's accident, Erika's eyes burned, and her throat swelled closed. For a moment, she couldn't do anything but blink to clear her eyes, not wanting to cry on the baby. But it was heartbreaking. April—young, beautiful, talented, reckless, rudderless April—was gone. Killed in a horrendous accident that had somehow left her baby unscathed. But now Beck was alone, having lost his mom, the only person he'd ever known.

Erika's gut cramped as she imagined April's mental and emotional state these past few months. Why hadn't April reached out to her? Erika would have been there for her. She would have moved April to Riverside, she would have gotten her help—she broke off, shook her head, the sharp pain in her stomach echoing the ache in her chest. It was too late for all of that, too late for April, but not for April's son.

As the infant's tiny fingers slipped around her fingertip and held on tightly, Erika vowed to do right by April's baby. *We'll find your dad*, she silently promised him, gazing down into his wide blue eyes. How could he not want you?

Chapter One

The need to discover the identity of Beck's father drove her as Erika cleaned and organized April's apartment, packing up clothes and making plans to donate all the furniture. Erika had been in Las Vegas for two days when she unearthed a box of photo books, the kind you made by uploading your pics and then getting a little bound book sent to you. One of the books was filled with photos from the weekend Erika had spent with April two years ago, pages filled with smiles and laughter as well as lots of food shots. They'd eaten out every meal and had snapped endless pics of food and drink. And then there was another photo book, this one filled with April and a handsome cowboy. Pictures of a rodeo with the handsome cowboy in chaps, pictures in a bar, pictures in bed, where a sheet barely covered his hips and all he wore was a sexy half-smile with a wicked glint in his eyes.

Dark blue eyes, like Beck.

Dark blond hair, like the sole wisp of hair on Beck's round head.

Could this rugged—naked—cowboy be Beck's dad?

She glanced down into the bassinette where Beck was

sleeping and an ache formed in her chest, an ache that filled her every time she thought of the baby's future. She wanted what was best for the baby, and she wasn't sure she was the best, but was a cowboy better?

But it wasn't her right to make that decision. She needed to find Beck's dad and see what he wanted for his son. First, she needed the cowboy's name, and then second, she needed to locate him.

Discovering both didn't take long, not after finding out there was a whole association of professional cowboys, and scrolling through the membership profiles online, she saw a photo of April's cowboy. His name was Billy Wyatt.

Googling his name pulled up pages of rodeo wins, as well as articles and interviews. Within hours, she knew far more about him than she ever wanted to know. He was one of four brothers, three who were world champions on the professional rodeo circuit, often competing together, especially in the team events. He'd been raised by his mother and grandfather on the Wyatt family ranch in Paradise Valley, Montana, after his father, an emerging rodeo star, had died in an accident with his younger brother, Samuel, also a fixture on the rodeo scene.

The Wyatt brothers were talented, successful cowboys, and as it turned out, Billy was competing at the Tucson rodeo this very weekend.

Her heart sped up, adrenaline flooding her veins, making her push away from the laptop keyboard.

Did she dare? Could she just go, show up, introduce herself? But then why not? She'd been trying to locate Beck's father for days. This was her chance.

But two days later, while she and Beck sat in her car in the Tucson rodeo and fairgrounds parking lot, waiting for the late-February rain to let up, she wasn't so sure this was the best plan. Not because of the rain—it wasn't a hard rain, and outside the temperature was relatively mild, and no one else seemed to mind the rain. Even though the rodeo wouldn't start for hours, the vast parking lot was nearly full and folks streamed toward the gates in boots and hats and some kind of waterproof layer. But rather, she was a little worried at her audacity. Just showing up unannounced could be a problem. Her announcement could backfire. Billy Wyatt could be unpleasant.

Erika glanced over her shoulder into the backseat where Beck was securely strapped into his car seat. She'd hung a small mirror on the headrest of the seat so she could see his face, and he was wide awake, his dark blue eyes gazing intently at the bold black-and-white pattern beneath the mirror, his little feet moving restlessly. How could anyone be unpleasant to Beck though? He was the sweetest, most gorgeous baby boy, and he deserved all the love in the world. But the world wasn't a just place. Goodness wasn't always rewarded, and bad guys often prospered.

"We're going to meet your dad today," she said, her voice breaking the silence. "Not sure how this will go."

Obviously, Beck didn't answer, but her stomach did a nervous flip and she felt queasy all the way through. It had seemed so logical to come here and find Billy Wyatt, but now that she was here, she felt overwhelmed by doubt. No, make that anxiety, as well as fear.

How did you just spring it on someone that he had a son?

But it had to be done, so that Beck could be settled and secure with his forever family, as Erika knew her side of the family wasn't it. She herself had spent the past ten years trying to distance herself from her family, wanting more from her future than what she'd known in her past.

Finally, the rain eased and sun peeked through the clouds, creating a hopeful golden glow above. Erika drew a breath and exhaled hard. If she was going to do this, she needed to do it now, before the rodeo began.

With a knit cap on his head for warmth and Beck secure in a baby carrier on her chest, she allowed her yellow rain slicker with the bright blue flowers to drape over the baby carrier, covering enough of Beck so that he'd be protected from the worst of the odd splatter, while still being able to breathe. Head down, watching the watery potholes, she reviewed her plan for tracking down Beck's father. She'd buy the cheapest ticket she could, most likely a seat in the bleachers, but she had no intention of actually sitting anywhere. The best place to find a cowboy was near the chutes, or the horses, or somewhere in that vicinity. Her biggest question was, would she be allowed in that area?

So intent on avoiding mud, Erika walked into a couple in front of her. She lifted her head to apologize but froze as the man's head turned and looked down at her.

It was him. Him. April's cowboy, Beck's dad, Billy Wyatt, but he wasn't alone, his arm wrapped around the shoulders of a very slim, very pretty brunette.

Erika had studied her cousin's photo book so many times, trying to memorize the cowboy's face, trying to imagine who he was, and how he could get April pregnant and then just disappear, that it was shocking—overwhelming—to see him in person. Anything she'd hoped to say to him died, her heart racing too hard, her entire body cold. Frozen.

She'd been determined to find him, and she had. But it had never crossed her mind that he would be with someone when she found him. "I'm sorry," she said, taking an unsteady step back, mud squelching beneath her shoes.

He gave her an easy smile, creases fanning at his eyes. Blue eyes, bright blue eyes, so like Beck's. "You okay?" he asked.

"My fault. I wasn't looking." Her gaze searched his face, all those carefully rehearsed words having deserted her. He was good-looking, very good-looking, even better looking in person than in photos. Erika didn't quite know what to do with that knowledge, nor did she know what to think of the brunette tucked close to his side, slender, young, and very happy to be at Billy's hip.

This wasn't the scenario she'd imagined. Billy Wyatt wasn't just a photo from an album, but a tall, ruggedly handsome, seriously handsome man—strong cheekbones, square clean-shaven jaw, piercing blue eyes, sensual lips—and he was not single. At least, not at the moment.

She glanced down at Beck, his head covered in a knit cap, his small body shrouded in her bright yellow rain jacket. Her heart fell, her stomach ached.

This wasn't the time.

This wasn't the place. Eyes burning, throat constricting, Erika turned around, and slowly returned to her car, trying to figure out her next move.

BILLY WAS HAVING a good year, a really good year, and was in the finals each weekend, resulting in big money. He and Tommy were both doing well, and their sibling rivalry brought the best in both of them—who would take top spot? Who'd have the best time, the best score, the biggest win? They were pushing each other hard, usually entering the same rodeo because they both wanted to be attending the important rodeos, the ones that offered big winnings since in the professional rodeo circuit it was about earnings, not just wins.

Billy hated taking a weekend off, but missing out on a weekend of competition wasn't as painful as it would normally be because Tommy was missing out, too. The two of them had headed home to Montana. It was Granddad's eighty-ninth birthday and they weren't going to miss that. Not for all the money in the world. Granddad had raised them. He was like their dad, and the Wyatt boys loved him dearly.

Billy and Tommy had arrived late last night, pulling in after dark. Sophie and Joe had dinner waiting, and after visiting for a couple hours, had gone to bed, only to be woken up early for this morning's ride. Granddad wanted to go inspect some of the fencing that might have been damaged from the rockslide on the far side of the property, which was another way of saying, Granddad just wanted his boys with him on a ride. Nothing made him happier than being in the saddle, on the ranch, with his four grandsons.

They'd been out for several hours when Billy's mom's voice came over the walkie-talkie, radioing that she needed Billy to return to the house. She needed Billy, and only Billy, and she wanted him now. They were all together when the static filled message came through, having taken a coffee break.

Granddad arched a brow as he sipped from his thermos. "Your mom doesn't sound happy," he said.

Granddad was a master of understatement. Their mom, Summer, had a bit of sharpness to her, and the boys never knew if it was due to the grief of losing their dad when they were all so young, or her arthritis that had crippled her in her early forties, but they loved her despite her prickly edges, aware that she loved them, and would fight for them always.

"What did you do, Billy?" Tommy asked, feet planted, thumbs hooked over his belt, beneath his open sheepskin coat.

Billy shook his head even as he pushed up his sleeve to check his watch. Eleven fifteen. He shook the sleeve down again. "No idea, but I better head down. Don't want to keep her waiting. It won't help her mood."

"I always worry when we all leave her," Sam said. "She could fall. Something could happen."

Oldest brother, Joe, screwed the cap back on his coffee thermos. "Sophie is down there, just a stone's throw from the house. Mom would call her if it was serious."

Billy nodded, agreeing with Joe, but he was antsy to return now, and he slid his thermos back into a saddlebag, and then untied the reins from the quaking aspen, its bright green foliage heralding spring in the Absaroka Mountains. A moment later he swung up into the saddle and gave a nod to his brothers. "See you back at the house." And then he nudged his horse into a canter.

It'd take him a good thirty minutes to get home from this point, plenty of time to consider all his sins. But nothing significant came to mind. He was financially solvent, happily single, competing well, very well, earning very good money. He couldn't think of anything he'd done, at least lately, that would ruffle Mom's feathers.

Billy stopped thinking about what-ifs, clearing his mind to focus on the ride down the mountain. It had started out as a beautiful day with a pale blue sky, wispy clouds and spring sunshine but in the past hour clouds had moved overhead and the wind had picked up. Nothing alarming, just typical Montana weather.

Nearing the two-story log cabin house, Billy spotted a small navy car in the circular gravel driveway. He didn't recognize the car, nor could think of anyone he knew with California plates. Billy frowned as he settled his horse into his stall, quickly unsaddling the gelding and giving him a rub down. Leaving the barn, he glanced at the car once more, this time noting the words UC Riverside on the license plate frame. Still no help. He was completely clueless, and somehow he didn't think Publishers Clearinghouse announced its sweepstakes winners with a little car from San Bernardino, California.

Billy entered the house through the kitchen door, walking in on his mom seated at the big table with a strange woman. His mom was holding a baby. Billy's stomach did a sharp nosedive, plummeting straight to the tips of his boots. He glanced at the lady, didn't know her, glanced back to his mom who was gently patting the baby on his back. His forehead furrowed even as icy adrenaline flooded his veins.

What was going on?

His mom glanced up, met his gaze, her expression devoid of all emotion. "There you are," she said evenly. "I was telling Erika it would take you about a half an hour, and it did."

He looked at this Erika, wondering what she was doing here, wondering why his mother was holding the baby, wondering what any of this had to do with him. But he revealed none of it in his expression.

Instead, he washed his hands at the kitchen sink, and then turned. "Anyone want coffee? Tea? I could put the kettle on."

"No, thank you," Erika said. "Your mom already offered."

His mother shook her head. "Now that you're here, I'm going to leave you two to talk."

Erika left her seat to take the baby, and then his mom slowly, carefully rose, reaching for her walker. "It was nice to meet you, Erika," she said, before making her way from the room, her walker making little clicking sounds of the hardwood floor.

It was quiet after his mother left. Billy retrieved a mug from the cupboard, and then filled it with coffee from the coffeepot, giving Erika time to speak. She didn't.

His gaze swept her and the baby. He didn't know her. Thank God. Baby wasn't his.

And then his attention was caught by a yellow coat hanging on a hook near the back door. Bright yellow coat with blue flowers.

He'd seen that coat before. And now that he was thinking about it, her face looked vaguely familiar, but why? Where? His brow creased, trying to remember.

He walked to the table, pulled a chair out and sat down across from her. "Have we met?"

She shifted the baby, setting him down on her lap, facing outward. "Not officially, no."

He circled the mug with his palm. It warmed his hand. "You look familiar."

"I bumped into you, a few weeks ago. At the Tucson rodeo."

And then it came to him. The parking lot. The rain. And the vivid yellow jacket with French blue flowers. But the memory shifted to a sense of mistrust. First Tucson, now here. Why?

"I remember you," he said flatly. "What can I do for you?"

"I—" Her lips parted, and she touched the tip of her tongue to her upper lip before looking up into his face, her eyes meeting his. "I'm sorry. This isn't easy."

"Maybe just say it."

"This is your son, Beck. Beck Wyatt."

Billy's gaze locked with hers, his expression hard, unsmiling. He stiffened, and gave her a long unsmiling look. "Not following."

"He's yours. Your son. Paternity will be legally established as soon as you take a DNA test—"

"Since we've never slept together, how is he mine?"

"You did sleep with someone. It just wasn't me." Glancing down, she gently, lightly ran her hand across the baby's bald head. "His mom is gone, which is why I've been trying to find you." She looked back up at him. "And, yes, I found you in Tucson, but you were with someone and it didn't seem right to… do this… there."

Tucson… who was he with? And then he remembered. Jenna. "Appreciate that."

"I went to the San Antonio Stock Show the next weekend, but you were with a redhead then. I quickly realized that I would probably not ever find you… alone." Her chin lifted. "So here I am."

"Persistent, aren't you?"

"I have to be. We have a child without a mom, in need of a dad—"

His eyes narrowed. "You don't look like social services."

"I'm not. I'm April's cousin."

April.

He immediately conjured a tall slim dancer from Las Vegas. A sexy wild thing. They'd dated for a bit. Had some good times together. "April Estes?" he asked.

Erika nodded. "She was a professional dancer—"

"From Vegas," he finished. "You said she's gone. What do you mean by that? She's taken off, or…"

"Or. April was killed in a car crash early February." Erika's voice cracked. "They say she died instantly. At least I hope so. Beck was in the car, but he wasn't hurt. April made mistakes, but at least she'd secured him properly in the car seat so he survived the crash. Only now he's alone."

Billy's attention shifted to the baby in her arms. The infant was ridiculously small, with a ridiculously big bald head and a round, pale moon face. "Why do you think he's mine?"

"Besides his name being Wyatt?"

"That's not his legal name—"

"It's on his birth certificate."

"Then it's a middle name, not his surname. Can't be. Not without me signing a birth certificate."

She said nothing for a moment, surprised. "You know how this works then?"

"I've always been careful. I always use protection."

"Something failed this time, because you're his dad."

He got up, walked to the sink, arms folded across his chest. "April told you this?"

"No. I've been digging through her things, trying to piece it together."

"Then you've pieced it wrong. There's no way the baby is mine."

"You weren't together in Tucson last year, for the rodeo?" Before he could answer, Erika added, "In case it's hard to remember that far back, I found a photo album she made. If you'll just hold him—" She rose and thrust the infant against his chest, leaving him there. "I'll show you."

Billy had instinctively wrapped an arm around the baby

when she'd pushed the child toward him, and now he watched as she went to the table and dug a small photo book from her oversized purse. She marched back toward him and opened the little book, flipping through pages filled with photos and captions. He couldn't read the captions but the photos were clearly of him and April. April looking sensational in snug jeans, boots, and a tight shirt. April in his cowboy hat. April with him, here at the fairgrounds. At a bar. At a restaurant. Kissing. Wrestling. Cuddling naked in bed. April wearing nothing but his hat.

He swallowed, glanced at the top of moon face's bald head and asked, "When was he born?"

"November thirtieth." The woman's gaze met his. "He would have been conceived during last year's Tucson rodeo."

"She could have been already pregnant or gotten pregnant right after."

"There was no one else in her life at the time. Just you."

"How do you know?"

Erika froze, his question catching her off guard. Interesting. So she wasn't as sure of herself as she thought. "April and I were not ever in a relationship. We just hooked up now and then."

"That hooking up now and then still created your little bundle of joy." Erika smiled, but it was a tight smile, and it didn't reach her eyes. Her voice hardened, each word short, sharp. "And he needs his dad. He has no one else."

"What about you?"

"I've temporarily been appointed a guardian, and I'd like to remain in his life, play the doting aunt, or whatever one would call me, but I'm not his mom, nor am I prepared to be, not when I'm single, a full-time grad student, unable to financially provide."

"I'm sorry. What is your name again?"

"Erika."

"Listen, Erika, I don't think he's mine, but, if he was, I would, of course, financially provide for him, but I live on the road. I live out of a trailer. My life is spent in parking lots of fairgrounds across the country—"

"Then you might need to make some changes to your life. Your son needs you."

"I just found out five minutes ago I might have a kid, and now you're telling me to drop everything?"

"I had to when they called and said April was gone, and the baby isn't even mine. Beck is yours—"

"I think you assume too much."

"Then let's just get the test done, and we'll have the answer you need."

She nodded at the baby beginning to squirm against his chest. "And the answer he needs, too."

"Erika, it's my granddad's birthday today and I'm only home for a few days. We can't do this here and now. Not in front of my family. It's not fair to them—"

"What about Beck?"

"He has no idea what we're discussing."

"So you're not going to introduce him to your family?"

"No. Not until we know, and there's no way to know definitely now. Tomorrow I'm back on the road, heading to Idaho and then Oregon and I'll find a place to take a paternity test this week. I'm sure there's somewhere I could hit on the way, but until we have paternity squared away, I'm not going to turn myself inside out, or put my family through unnecessary drama, not without proof that that baby is mine."

"You don't believe me?"

"I don't believe April." He returned the baby to her, carefully, but firmly. "I can promise you I wasn't the only one she was seeing. April told me about some of the others."

Her jaw dropped. She adjusted Beck in her arms. "Why would she do that?"

He shrugged. "Make me jealous."

"Did it work?"

"I feel like we're going down the wrong path with this conversation, so I'm going to walk you to your car, see you off, and we can talk more tomorrow."

"Once you're on the road."

"Yes."

"You're running away."

"No, not running away. But I can promise you one thing, we're not going to continue this here, now—" Billy broke off as the kitchen door opened and laughter filled the kitchen as his brothers trooped in. He shot Erika a hard look, his expression fierce. "Not a word, not to any of them."

ONE MINUTE IT was just Billy and her, and the next, the kitchen was full of Wyatt men—one cowboy after another, the vintage kitchen alive with deep, masculine voices, broad shoulders, and intense testosterone. The brothers, clearly they were all brothers except for the grandfather, had a remarkable family resemblance, with thick hair ranging from dark gold to a sun-kissed brown. Their eyes were all light, and they each had the same features, strong jaws, straight noses, high cheekbones. Looking at the older man, she could see they'd inherited their rugged good looks from him, as he was the same, only more weathered with silver hair and piercing blue eyes.

The boisterous Wyatts drew up short when they spotted her. She knew the moment each noticed the baby, as their expressions changed, one by one, from open to surprised to guarded. She felt much the same facing them and her heart raced, making her feel anxious all over.

"Don't mind me," she said brightly, trying to hide her nerves, and just how much Billy had rattled her. "I'm on my way out."

One of the brothers looked to Billy, but Billy said nothing.

She lifted her purse, which also served as a diaper bag, and headed for the door, stepping between the cluster of men. As she lifted her cheerful yellow, flower-strewn coat, the older man spoke, his voice deep, almost gruff. "No need to rush away. Nice to have visitors up here."

"She's got to get back to town," Billy said flatly, again giving her that same don't-try-me look. "The baby needs to eat and nap." His gaze locked with hers, the blue in his eyes almost icy. "It's what you'd said, right?"

She stared into his eyes, anxiety fading, anger growing. Who did he think he was? She held his gaze another moment, letting him know she wasn't intimidated, or impressed. He didn't care about his son or April. He didn't seem to care for anyone but himself.

"Not exactly," she answered, not bothering to smile or soften her tone. "But I will go, as you've asked, and since you've promised to call me in the morning, I look forward to speaking to you then."

Erika then looked to the others, nodding stiffly at the circle of men, hating the lump filling her throat. "Goodbye," she said, before glancing at the senior Wyatt, the one Billy said was celebrating his birthday today. "Happy birthday, Mr. Wyatt. I hope it's a happy one." Then she opened the door, stepped out, and closed it firmly behind her.

It had grown cold and windy while she'd been in the house, steely clouds blanketing the sky, hiding the sun. Jaw tight, Erika buckled Beck into his car seat, hating the hot emotions rushing through her, making her feel too many things. She was angry and appalled. She'd known Billy was a playboy, a man who had a woman in every town at every rodeo, but she'd expected him to be a little more interested in his son.

How could April have fallen for him? What had she seen in him? Other than a handsome face and lean, muscular body?

The mudroom door opened and Billy appeared on the back porch. Erika shot him a look of pure disdain as she walked around the car to the driver's side.

"Hold up," he said.

She arched an eyebrow. "Excuse me?"

"Could you *please* wait?" he replied, closing the distance between them.

She tugged her coat closer. "Why?"

"My grandfather would like you to join us for dinner."

She stood even straighter. "Why?"

"It's his birthday."

"No, I know that. But why would he want me to join you for dinner? Did you say something to him?"

"No. What would you want me to say?"

"That there is a very good chance that Beck is your baby, and your grandfather's great-grandson."

"Not going to do that until we know for sure."

"Because it'd get his hopes up?"

"Because my brother Joe and his wife Sophie are expecting a baby late spring, the first Wyatt grandbaby for my mother, and I'm not going to steal Joe and Sophie's thunder, not unless it's absolutely essential."

"Seems like everybody's feelings are more important than a four-month-old baby's needs.

His jaw tightened. "You're a stranger, and you show up on our doorstep with a baby and a photo book, claiming I'm its dad—"

"He's not an it. Beck is a person, a boy—"

"And you don't expect me to be suspicious? I'm supposed to believe whatever you say without any proof?"

"What do I gain by making false claims?"

He shrugged. "Money."

Stunned, revolted, she stepped back, bumping hard into the mirror on the side of her car. "Wow. Did you really just say that?"

He shrugged. "It wouldn't be the first time."

"Maybe you should keep your junk in your pants then—"

"I wasn't talking about me."

Her face burned hot but she held his icy-blue gaze, unable to remember when she was last so angry. "Please apologize to your grandfather, but I can't stay. I have a room booked in town, at the Bramble House, and maybe after your dinner, you can spare me five minutes of your incredibly valuable time."

"You make it very difficult to have a conversation with you."

"Whereas you're just not ever available for a conversation."

"Can I just say that your hostility—" He broke off as two women came into view, walking up the road, one with dark brown hair and visibly pregnant carrying packages, while the other, a slim brunette in tight jeans and boots, held a cake stand with an extravagantly frosted birthday cake.

Erika felt the scrutiny of the women as they approached. Her chin notched up a fraction, even as her stomach did a flip-flop. She felt anxious and defensive and hated it. "That's a beautiful cake," she said, forcing a smile.

The woman carrying the cake nodded to the pregnant woman. "Sophie made it. She's our resident baker."

"Hope you're staying to have some," Sophie said. "We have plenty." She gave the packages to Billy and extended her hand. "I'm Sophie Wyatt, Joe's wife. Welcome to the Diamond W Ranch."

"Erika Baylor," Erika answered, grateful for Sophie's friendliness. "I met your husband inside." She looked at the cowgirl with the cake. "And probably yours?"

"Sam," the cowgirl answered, one of her long braids slipping over her shoulder. "I'm Ivy Wyatt. We don't live here, just visiting for the day. I'm going to get the cake inside, but please don't rush away. Sophie and I love when we can add more girls to the mix. Balances out some of the intense male energy." She started for the cabin and then paused. "Billy, bring Granddad's presents in. Let Sophie have a moment with Erika while you and I set the table."

Billy's mouth open, closed. He glowered at Ivy, who

simply arched an eyebrow, not at all intimidated. Erika was impressed. And not just with Ivy, but Sophie, too. Clearly these women knew how to handle their men.

Billy shot her an indecipherable look, before following Ivy up the porch and into the house.

As the door shut behind Billy, Sophie gave Erika a bright smile. "He can be charming."

Erika couldn't find it in her to smile back. "What have you heard, if anything?"

"That there was a possible Wyatt baby sighting." Sophie patted her round stomach. "Other than this one."

Heat rushed through Erika. "I didn't say anything to the others—"

"You didn't have to. According to Joe, he looks like a Wyatt baby."

"What does a Wyatt baby look like?"

"Take a peek in the hall. There are framed photos of every Wyatt baby going back three generations." Sophie gave her a curious look. "Unless Joe has it wrong?"

"I don't think so." Erika saw Sophie's expression and added, "He's my cousin's baby, not mine, and she's gone. I'm trying to find Beck's dad."

"And you think Beck's dad is Billy?"

Erika nodded. "But then, I might have put two and two together and gotten five, which is why I'm here to ask Billy to take a DNA test."

"Sounds fair."

"Only my timing is terrible. I didn't mean to crash Mr. Wyatt's party, or to..." She swallowed hard, finding the words uncomfortable. "Or, take away from your baby—"

"You're not taking away from my baby. He—or she—is snug as a bug here." Sophie gave her tummy a little rub. "But it does seem like a long way to go to find Bill. He's not here often."

"I know, but one of the girls dating Tommy heard that Billy and Tommy would be at the family ranch this weekend, so I piled us in the car and headed north." Erika glanced into the backseat of the car. "Billy's hard to get alone. He almost always has… company."

Sophie's brown gaze glinted with humor, as well as something else. "He's popular."

She crossed to the open door of the car and peeked in at the sleeping baby. "You said his name is Beck?"

"Beck Wyatt Estes. He was born last November, right before Thanksgiving."

"And his mom? She's passed?"

"She died in a car accident a month ago."

"I'm sorry."

Sophie sounded sincere and Erika appreciated it. It had bothered Erika that the world didn't seem to care that April was gone. Erika knew the world could be a hard and brutal place, but this absence of grief for her cousin wounded her. "April had kept the arrival of the baby to herself. No one in our family knew. I only knew when the police called me, notifying me that she'd been killed and I was her emergency contact."

"How awful, and how tragic for Beck to lose his mom that way."

Emotion thickened Erika's chest, making it hard to swallow, and impossible to speak. She blinked hard, clearing the burning sensation from her eyes. She'd felt together, strong, until now. Sophie's sympathy was proving to be her undoing. "He hasn't had the easiest start in life," she agreed hoarsely.

"You two both need to come inside and relax. We have a big dinner planned for Granddad. Brisket, ribs, and pulled pork. There's a lot of food, and always room at the Wyatt table."

Erika looked to the old two-story cabin, thinking of Billy's expression as he walked away. "I don't think everyone wants us here."

"This is Melvin's house, not Billy's, and it's Melvin's birthday, not Billy's. And Melvin and Summer want you here. And so do I. Please stay, at least for dinner? There's no need for you to hustle down the mountain if you have nowhere specific to be."

Again Erika blinked back the sting of hot salty tears. She was tired, no, make that exhausted, and the idea of being with people, kind people, even just for a bit, was certainly appealing. "If you're sure no one would mind"—she broke off, made a face—"other than Billy."

"No one minds, and I bet Billy doesn't, either. He's just… surprised. And let's face it; the news that he could be a daddy to that baby boy is huge. It's news that could change his life forever."

AN HOUR LATER, Erika was fast asleep in a big, winged chair in the Wyatt living room, while Ivy, Sophie, and Sam took turns carrying the baby around. Erika had protested that she wasn't tired, but when she sat down to give Beck a bottle, she fell asleep, and Beck didn't. Sam eased the baby out of Erika's arms, Ivy covered her with a blanket, and they all let her be to catch up on some much-needed sleep.

Granddad peeked in at one point and then left, remarking to Billy that, "she reminds me a little of Goldilocks."

Billy had no reply to that, not at all comfortable with how protective his family was being of Erika and the baby. There was a very good chance that the baby wasn't his and it worried him that they were all getting a little too attached.

While dinner cooked, Summer pulled Billy aside, speaking to him in the den. "So what are you going to do?" she asked her son, sinking into her recliner.

Billy chose not to sit, and he shrugged, fighting back his irritation. "Take a paternity test, figure it out."

"I think it's smart to get a paternity test, but I can tell you right now, that is your baby. That, or one of your brothers."

Billy's head swiveled, his narrowed gaze meeting his mom's. "You're reaching, Mom."

Her lips pursed, her gaze sharp. "That's a Wyatt baby, Bill. I've had four of them, and that's what you all looked like. Round bald heads, peaches and cream skin, big blue eyes, happy smiles. You came out looking like cherubs. Not sure why, because once you grew up, you weren't angelic creatures."

"Thanks, Mom." He paced the room, his shoulders hunching as he approached the window, his gaze going to the view of the barn and stables beyond. "If it's mine, it will change everything."

"Babies generally do." His mom leaned back in her chair, hands folding on her lap. "That baby needs a home. It's your responsibility now to give him that home. It might be time to retire—"

"Lots of guys compete with families. Sometimes the families go on the road, sometimes they waited home—"

"You have a baby without a mama. Who's going to take care of your baby while you travel? Certainly not my job, not your granddad's job, not any of your brothers' job—"

"We don't even know if that baby is mine."

"Then go to Marietta tomorrow and take a test. I'm sure there's a lab at the hospital that does paternity tests."

"Tomorrow's Sunday."

"Then go Monday."

"I need to get on the road Monday."

"Yes, you do. Right after you take the test."

Billy closed his eyes and pressed two fingers to his brow, pressing back against the dull thudding pain that had been there all evening. "I know you're angry, and disappointed—"

"Mistakes happen, Bill. It's what you do after the mistake, that's what I'm concerned about."

He gave her a fierce look. "I know my responsibilities. If Beck is mine, I'm taking him with me. I won't be leaving him behind or pawning him off on someone else. If he's my son, I'll be the one raising him."

"Good. That's all I wanted to hear."

Chapter Two

No one even mentioned the snow, not during dinner, or over cake and coffee while Melvin opened the gifts his grandsons had for him. It wasn't until Erika had risen at the very end of the meal and helped carry dishes into the kitchen that she noticed the strange lavender white light outside. It was night, and dark, but the kitchen window over the sink revealed a pale glow. She leaned closer to the window and stared out, taking a moment to realize it was snow. Thick, white snow covering everything.

Tommy joined her at the sink, scraping the remnants of cake off the dessert plates before tackling the plates she'd carried in. "It's been coming down steadily all evening," he said.

"I had no idea," she answered.

He submerged all the plates in the hot soapy water filling the sink. "If you don't have four-wheel drive, you might be stuck here tonight."

She frowned. "Surely it's not that bad."

"Go have a look."

Erika exited the mudroom door and stepped out onto

the porch, taking in the landscape that now was white. The thick snowflakes were still falling, a steady silent flurry from the sky. She glanced at Sophie and Joe who'd joined her outside on the porch. "It's beautiful," she said, her voice low, a hint of wonder in her voice.

"Another California girl," Joe said, wrapping his arm around his wife's shoulders.

"I still love it," Sophie said with a smile. "But after a year, I've learned all the downsides. Fortunately, we don't have to drive anywhere tonight, not like Sam and Ivy."

"Or, Erika," Joe added, looking to Erika. "It's going to be tough for you to get down the mountain tonight."

"That's what Tommy said," she answered, chewing her bottom lip. "I don't suppose there are four-wheel drive Ubers—"

"Come in, and close the door," Summer called from the house. "It's cold. No need to heat the outdoors."

Sophie and Joe exchanged quick smiles even as they headed back in. Erika followed them, feeling somewhat scolded. But returning to the kitchen she found Summer seated at the kitchen table, rocking the baby carrier that had been placed on the table. Beck was awake and gazing up at all the people in the room.

"Had you checked into a motel yet?" Summer asked Erika.

Erika shook her head. "Not yet. I have a reservation in Marietta, but we came straight here. I hadn't expected to be here so long."

"Have you paid for the room yet?"

"No, but they're holding it—"

"That's fine. We'll call and get it canceled. You'll stay here tonight." Summer gestured to Tommy. "Go bring in their luggage. Get the keys, find out what they need." She looked at Billy. "Billy, show them to Sam's room and point out where everything is. Make sure she gets fresh towels and you might need to turn on the little heater that's in the closet, to make sure Sam's room warms up."

"That's really not necessary," Erika protested weakly. "I appreciate the offer of hospitality, but the last thing I want to do is—"

"No trouble at all," Summer interrupted. "It's dangerous driving and that little baby doesn't need another accident."

Erika opened her mouth to protest, but closed it without saying anything, because Mrs. Wyatt had made an excellent point. Beck had survived one deadly crash. The last thing he needed was another tragedy. "Perhaps I could go with Sam and Ivy… aren't they heading down to town soon?"

"They're heading to their ranch, but it's the opposite direction of Marietta. No sense putting them in harm's way, either."

Erika nodded, because of course Summer Wyatt was right. "I wouldn't want to do that, no."

"I can drive her down in my truck, Mom," Billy said, his deep voice pitched even lower. "Tommy and I could get her car down to her sometime in the morning."

"That's a good idea," Erika said quickly, latching onto the possibility.

"Unless it doesn't stop snowing and then she's trapped without a car, and she can't go hiking around town with a baby without any snow gear." Summer's brow creased as she looked at Erika, even as she continued rocking the car seat. "Did you bring snow gear?"

Erika shook her head. "It's, uh, almost April."

"It can snow here until May," Tommy said, from his position leaning against the stove. "The day can start out hot and sunny and still end in wind and snow."

"Let's not discuss weather. Let's get our guest settled," Summer said. "Tommy, Billy, please?"

Billy nodded, not about to argue with his mom, but he didn't know why his mom was so insistent on Erika and the baby staying when she'd always been firmly against any pretty single woman staying over.

Nevertheless, he waited while she retrieved her car keys for Tommy before lifting the car seat from the kitchen table and carrying it with him as he led the way upstairs to a room halfway down the hall. Billy pushed open Sam's door and flipped on the light. The room *was* distinctly chilly. He placed the baby and car seat on the floor and walked to the closed ceiling vent, opening it, but there was no encouraging gust of heat. It'd take considerable time for the room to warm up. As if reading his mind, Erika stopped him before he'd gone to the closet.

"I can plug the heater in," she said. "You don't need to trouble yourself further. Just tell me where I'd find a couple of towels and a bathroom and I'll be fine."

"The bathroom is next door. Sam and Joe used to share it but since neither are here anymore, it's all yours. There should be clean towels under the sink." He hesitated. "What about the baby? Does he need anything?"

"The travel crib in the car trunk. It's stored in a large black backpack."

"I'll go get it. Anything else while I'm going that way?"

"I have a large water bottle by the driver's seat. It's red with bright orange and pink flowers."

He returned a few minutes later with the backpack and water bottle. He could see that Tommy had already brought up the rest of her things. She'd also plugged the heater in and turned it on. It hadn't warmed the room yet but the night was cold and it'd take a while. "I'm going to grab you an extra quilt," he said. "And then I'll set up the crib if you'd like."

"I can do it."

"I don't mind lending a hand."

She gave him a strained smile. "I'm fine, thank you." She crossed to her purse and diaper bag and pulled a little photo album from one of the bags. "But I shouldn't have this. For all I know, it was meant for you."

He didn't want the photo book, and he tried to hand it

back but she wouldn't take it and it'd be rude to just leave it on the bed.

He left her room and went to his, a room he'd shared with Tommy since they were both in cribs, and setting the photo book down on his dresser he headed into his bathroom, stripping off his clothes and stepping into the shower. The water came out cold, little ice needles raining down, but Billy forced himself to stand there, finding a strange solace in the brutally cold shower. Anything was better than looking at that small square book Erika had thrust into his hand as she said good night to him.

He didn't need a book to remember April, and he didn't need photos to picture her. She'd been fun and she'd had a wild streak, enjoying cutting loose with him—drinking, dancing, not vanilla lovemaking. But there had never been feelings between them, much less serious feelings, nor were they ever in a relationship.

From the beginning, she was seeing different guys—there had even been a sugar daddy from New Jersey that visited her in Vegas—and he'd been clear he was seeing other women, too. They'd agreed that they weren't into commitments, and even if they were, long-distance relationships didn't work. Far better to just meet up when convenient, than have hard and fast rules. He'd put April on the rodeo pass list more than once, happy to see her when she showed up at one of his events, and then they'd always hang out after, but she wasn't the only one he did that for. While he didn't have a woman in every town, there was a handful he enjoyed seeing when he was in their town.

The shower finally turned warm and Billy lifted his face to the spray. He wasn't going to apologize for liking women. He'd never apologize for that. He was single, thirty, and in the prime of his career. What was wrong with enjoying himself? Why shouldn't he have a pretty girl to kill time with?

He wasn't going to apologize for not loving any of them, either. It wasn't that he went out of his way to not fall in love. He just didn't. And he didn't know why. To be honest, he was rather on the fence about the whole falling-in-love thing anyway. If it wasn't for Joe and Sam, he'd doubt that romantic love existed at all. Joe had a serious girlfriend back in high school, a girl from Marietta named Charity, and he'd been head over heels for her, and now he had Sophie and he loved her, too.

Sam and Ivy had a completely different love—the kind that just wouldn't go away—even when they were apart for years. Now that they were back together, they were inseparable, traveling on the circuit together, training horses together, working with young riders together. It was as if they couldn't function without the other and Billy had never once felt that way about anyone. He and Tommy had even talked about it, and Tommy said that although he wasn't ready to settle down, he looked forward one day to having a family.

Not Billy.

Family meant commitments and responsibilities he didn't want. Not now, not ever.

He turned the water off, stepped from the shower, water sluicing down his body and reached for a towel, taking his time drying off, enjoying the brisk rubdown.

So what if Beck was his?

What if the baby in the next room was his son?

Billy lifted the towel, dried his hair and then covered his face with the towel, and drew a deep breath, trying to process it all.

My God, if he was Beck's dad, everything had just changed. Forever.

It was a strange thing to think about, being a father, possibly having a son, aware he was nowhere near ready to be a decent father. He was strong, fit, able to do things physically most men could never do, but take care of another human being? Never mind a helpless little thing that could barely hold his head up on his own? Billy shuddered. Now that was danger.

Being the third son meant you were the third in line for everything—clothes, food, opportunities. But it also meant that you had fewer responsibilities. Joe had always shouldered the most work and most of their mother's grief when Dad died. Sam had taken on what Joe needed help with. That left Billy and Tommy free to screw around and do what they wanted to do, which generally meant have a good time.

And they did have a good time. They loved life. They loved their freedom and their career and their success. Good Lord, they'd been successful, earning more money than either of them knew what to do with—well, not true. Tommy knew. Tommy was the one with the head for numbers. He was the Wyatt everyone talked to when needing investment advice. Tommy understood the stock market, he understood economics. If he'd gone to college, he'd probably be working on Wall Street now. He was that smart, that good at math, that good at equations, predictions, statistics.

Billy didn't have a talent like Tommy's, or a passion for ranching like Sam and Joe. The only thing he was really good at was riding, roping, competing. He was a damn good cowboy, a risk taker, a winner. But take him off the road, take away his horse, and he had nothing to offer. Nothing but charm and sex. That was his talent. He knew how to make a woman feel good in bed. He'd known that since he was sixteen.

But being good in bed was exactly what had gotten him into this situation now.

❦

ERIKA SLOWLY CIRCLED the bedroom, Beck tucked under her chin, held closely against her chest.

She'd wrapped the extra quilt from her bed around both of them, trying to keep warm. Beck was having a hard time tonight, far more fretful than he'd been in weeks. He'd woken up just after midnight crying, and he'd spent the last two hours alternating between whimpers and cries, and so she kept picking him up and trying to calm him, not wanting Beck's cries to wake up everyone else. It was an old house and she imagined sound traveled far too well.

She peered at her wristwatch, the green time glowing in the dark. Three thirty-eight. She'd been walking him for hours now, and she didn't know what to do next. He'd been fed over an hour ago, and changed, and he didn't feel feverish, but something was making him fretful and she was just feeling helpless and useless.

Erika did another little loop around her room, pausing at the window to lift the curtain and look out. The snow had stopped falling, and the moon glowed bright, reflecting off the thick layers of white. Everywhere she looked was frosted in snow—pine branches, porch overhang, fences, the trucks and her car in the driveway. She had never seen so much snow in her life. No wonder the room was so cold, and maybe that was the reason that Beck couldn't sleep. Maybe he was too cold. Personally, she was freezing, even in socks with a quilt around her shoulders. The little heater in the closet didn't put out much heat and she hadn't wanted to complain but now she regretted not speaking up.

Maybe the kitchen would be warmer. Maybe she could even make something warm to drink. Drawing the quilt more close, she opened the door and made her way to the top of the stairs, where she flipped on the light and carefully made her way down with Beck crying as if there was no tomorrow.

In the kitchen, she turned on the light over the stove and then lit the burner beneath the kettle and then walked, and hummed to Beck, bouncing him ever so gently even though all she wanted to do was put him down and walk away.

How did parents do this? How did single moms do this? Her patience was shot. Her eyes burned hot and gritty. Even her shoulders and back ached.

Maybe Beck was hungry now. Rather than go back upstairs to retrieve the bottle, she made him another one from the formula and bottle on the counter, placing the bottle in the same little pan she'd used earlier to heat his bottle.

He wailed while they waited for the bottle to warm.

He wailed while she tested the temperature of the milk on the inside of her wrist.

He wailed when she put the bottle to his mouth, turning his head away, small fists waving furiously.

Why was he so miserable? Was it possible he was teething, or was he too young? She didn't think he had a fever, but couldn't be sure. She patted his diapered backside and it still felt dry. She tried the bottle again, and once more, he turned his face away, his little mouth and eyes screwing up for another sharp wail.

"Come on, little guy, come on, Beck. Work with me. I don't know what I'm doing, either. I don't know how to make you feel better."

The kettle started to hiss, and she turned the gas off before it came to a full boil. She couldn't fill her cup, not when Beck was arching and crying, and there was nowhere to put him down. Tea was a bad idea.

Coming here had been a bad idea.

She should have simply sent Billy a letter, giving him the facts, and asking him to meet her somewhere.

She should have avoided all of this.

And actually, she could have. She didn't have to take Beck. She could have left him with social services. They would have put him in foster care and then eventually found a family for him. It was what they would have done if they hadn't reached Erika, or if she'd refused to come to Las Vegas.

But she'd chosen to go to Las Vegas. She'd rushed there, and she'd wanted to take him. She'd wanted to honor April's wishes, but right now, she felt useless. Useless, not hopeless, but still, incredibly discouraged.

She blinked, trying to make her eyes stop burning. But blinking just made her throat grow tighter and her chest feel heavier. She couldn't remember when she last felt so overwhelmed. She hated feeling helpless, and her nerves were stretched tight from all the crying. There was such a sharp pitch to a baby's cry, high, painful, demanding attention. "Beck," she whispered, "please. Tell me what's wrong. Come on, baby. Help me out here."

BILLY WOKE UP in the night, a high piercing sound penetrating his dream. Eyes open, he listened intently. A wail. Then another. And another.

It was April's baby.

But April was gone.

He hadn't known what to feel earlier, shock overriding everything else, but now, in the dark of night, he felt sorrow and sympathy for a child that had lost his mother. It was a terrible thing to lose a parent. Billy had been just three when his dad and his uncle Samuel were killed in the accident on the way to the rodeo in Deadwood. Billy didn't remember his dad, but there had been plenty of photos to show him who his dad had been, as well as how much his dad had loved his boys.

Was Beck *his* boy?

Billy struggled to wrap his mind around the possibility. Parenthood had been the last thing on his mind. He wasn't interested in marriage, had no desire to settle down, and children weren't part of the plan—maybe ever. If he did have kids, he'd known it would be years from now, when he'd gotten the hunger for competition out of his blood. But that wasn't now. He loved everything about being a professional cowboy, loved all of it—the travel, the events, the time with his brothers, as well as the evenings with the pretty women who lined up for a dance, or a kiss, or more.

April had been one of those. She was fun, flirty, playful in bed. But she'd never be the one, and he'd never made bones about the fact that he wasn't looking for more than a good time. It sounded crass, put that way, but it was the truth, and he was nothing but honest with the women he got naked with.

Could their crazy nights have created Beck?

And if so, why hadn't April reached out to him?

Why not let Billy know he had a kid?

Regardless, a baby was wailing away down in the kitchen and Billy wasn't going to be able to sleep now. He eased from bed, dressed warmly, and headed downstairs.

The kitchen was dark, with just the light on over the stove to illuminate the space. Billy spotted Erika near the door in the mudroom, facing the coatrack and swaying side to side, her hand slowly rubbing the baby's small back. He watched her a long moment, thinking she looked impossibly tired. He could feel her exhaustion from across the room.

"How long have you been up?" he asked quietly, not wanting to startle her.

She turned quickly, startled anyway. "Did his crying wake you?"

"It's not a big deal."

"I came down here so we wouldn't wake your mom or grandfather."

"That was thoughtful of you."

"But you're awake."

"It's okay. I'm a fairly light sleeper," he answered, crossing the kitchen floor. "But don't worry about Tommy. He sleeps like the dead."

"Do you know what time it is? I left my watch upstairs."

"Three thirty, maybe."

"I can't get him to stop crying."

"Does he have a fever?"

"I don't think so. Maybe he's just overstimulated. It was a big day."

"All those Wyatts are enough to terrify even the most manly of men." Billy smiled crookedly. "Let me take him, and you go back to bed." He'd reached her side and lifted the baby from her arms without waiting for her to answer.

Erika didn't protest. If anything, she looked grateful. "Normally, I'd ask if you were sure, but I'm so tired. I can hardly keep my eyes open."

"Then don't. Go to bed. Get sleep. I've got him."

Uncertainty flickered over her features. "Do you know anything about babies?"

"No, but I've delivered foals and calves, and given nearly every animal a bottle, from kittens to lambs and even a fawn Granddad found after his mom had been shot by hunters trespassing on our property."

Her fist pressed to her mouth. "What happened to the fawn?"

"We raised him until he could manage on his own."

"Did he?" she asked. "Manage on his own?"

"We think he's the big buck that comes around sometimes, and stands at the edge of the property looking at us.

We've gotten close to him a couple of times, but then he leaves. I'm pretty sure that's Rudy."

"Rudy?"

"As in Rudolph. Tommy named him."

The corner of her mouth curved as she gave him a sweet sleepy smile. "I have a feeling you guys are full of stories."

"So many," he agreed. "Too many. But now, go sleep. And you don't have to worry about Beck and me. I can manage giving a baby a bottle, and if I need you, I will get you."

"I've made a bottle up for him already. It's on the counter by the stove, but Beck didn't want it. He's just cranky tonight. Sometimes I wonder if he's missing his mom." Her voice cracked. "And then I want to cry."

"That's because you're thinking too much. It's never good to overthink, not in the middle of the night. Go to bed, sleep. Things will be better in the morning."

She pushed a heavy wave of golden hair back from her cheek, even as her troubled gaze met his. "Will they? He still won't have a mom, and I'm not sure he has a dad—"

"Stop. If I'm his dad, he has a dad. I'm going to take the test, and will know the truth soon, and then with facts in hand, we will come up with a plan."

"What if you're not the father?"

"I thought you were pretty confident I was."

"I wouldn't have driven this far if I didn't think so."

"Then don't torture yourself anymore tonight. Get sleep

and we can discuss this, and whatever else you want tomorrow."

Her gaze clung to his, deep purple shadows etched beneath her eyes, revealing her fatigue. "Promise?"

"I promise."

※

DESPITE BEING UTTERLY exhausted, Erika couldn't fall asleep right away. Her room was still chilly and she shivered under the covers, head pounding, eyes dry. She drew her knees up to her chest, trying to get warm, but instead of drifting off, she kept picturing Billy in the kitchen with the baby, the infant tiny against his big shoulder, and it made her insides do an uncomfortable wobble. She had such mixed feelings about Billy Wyatt, discovering quickly he was hard, self-absorbed, and uncaring. She'd decided she didn't like him, or respect him, but then he'd appeared in the kitchen in the dead of night to take care of a baby he wasn't convinced was his. He didn't have to come downstairs. He could have remained in bed and pretended he didn't hear the crying. But he didn't, and that changed her assumptions about him.

Not completely, but just enough for her to realize she didn't want to like him. It was easier to resent him for getting April pregnant and then disappearing on her. It felt good to be angry with him. She wanted to be angry with someone. April deserved more kindness in life, more support. But neither April, nor she, had been born into a family that offered unconditional love. Their family had rigid views based on a very strict faith. Step out of the faith and you were punished. April and Erika's mothers, sisters, had been banished. It wasn't until April's mom returned to the family, and the church, that she was forgiven. April hadn't wanted that life for her and she'd paid the price.

Covers pulled tightly to her chin, Erika remembered dinner tonight and the boisterous Wyatt men around the table. They'd teased each other mercilessly during the meal, and their laughter had made their mother smile, albeit somewhat reluctantly. Summer was rather reserved, and yet she'd been kind to Erika, and her sons clearly loved her. This was the kind of family Erika had seen on TV shows, the kind of family that had made her want more from life, that made her want to help others to want, and have, more for herself.

If Beck was a Wyatt, he'd be loved. Deeply loved.

A lump filled Erika's throat and she squeezed her eyes closed, overwhelmed by emotions she didn't really understand, because this was what she wanted for April's baby. She pictured Beck downstairs, nestled against Billy's broad chest, and felt yet another pang. Erika could see why her cousin had fallen for the Montana cowboy. He was ridiculously handsome, as well as tall, muscular, rugged, strong. He was a man's man, which women would love.

But why hadn't April told Billy about the baby?

Why had she kept it secret from Billy?

Was it possible she wasn't sure Beck was Billy's?

Had Erika possibly gotten it wrong... that Billy wasn't the father? Her heart fell and she rolled onto her back, and stared up at the beamed ceiling.

If he wasn't, what then? Where did Erika even begin to track down Beck's real father?

Worn out, she told herself to stop thinking, at least for tonight. The best thing to do was take it all one step at a time. Have Billy take the DNA test. Discover the truth.

And maybe pray that Billy was the father, because the Wyatts were good people. They were a close family, and yes, filled with testosterone, but they'd protect Beck, and they'd do right by him, not just now, but always.

And with that thought in mind, she finally fell asleep.

IT HAD BEGUN snowing again sometime in the night, creating a glorious winter wonderland—at least for those who could stay in the cabin. Melvin and his grandsons all had chores to do, and Erika came down to the kitchen in search of Beck, and found him asleep in Summer's arms. Summer was seated at the kitchen table while the Wyatt men were lounging in various positions around the kitchen, discussing their strategy for the morning. Joe and Granddad would tend to the livestock. Billy and Tommy would snowplow the roads. The snow had fallen most of the night and it'd take all day to get the road down to the public highway snowplowed, and that was even with Joe later taking a turn at the wheel.

Conversation momentarily broke off when Erika entered the kitchen but after pointing her to the coffeepot, the third pot of the day, freshly brewed, discussion resumed. Erika sat down with her coffee at the table, whispering to Summer that she could take Beck.

Summer shook her head. "It's nice to hold a baby again," she said softly.

Erika's chest felt warm and rather tender. Again, she thought how lucky Beck would be if this was his family, even as she worried that maybe she'd gotten it wrong. Maybe she'd gotten Summer's hopes up, and created conflict that wasn't necessary.

The men headed out shortly, and Erika spent the morning with Beck, feeding him when he woke up, then giving him a bath in the kitchen sink, before putting him in clean warm clothes.

Mrs. Wyatt invited Erika to join her in the den while she gave Beck an early lunch bottle. "The chairs are more comfortable," Summer said, easing herself into her own recliner. "This is where we spend our evenings, but every now and then I like to come in here and just sit a bit. It's warm in here, and quieter."

Taking a seat on the leather covered couch, Erika nuzzled Beck's warm sweet head. He smelled impossibly delicious—at least at this moment, after his bath, his small body in a fresh soft onesie, wrapped in an equally soft blanket. "It is nice in here," she said, appreciating the old cast-iron wood stove in the corner, making the room toasty. "But if I'm not careful, I might fall asleep."

"I wouldn't be surprised. I heard Beck kept you up most of the night."

"Until Billy came and saved me." Erika paused, trying to ignore the weird wobbly sensation in her middle that she felt every time she pictured Billy and Beck together. "That was nice of him."

Summer Wyatt leveled her gaze at Erika. "You think Billy's the baby's father?"

Erika suddenly found herself struggling to answer. She'd been so sure when she'd made the trip here. But now… now… she was worried she'd possibly muddled things up.

Erika needed a moment, and then chose her words carefully. "I'd thought so when I drove here, and I still think he could be. The timing makes sense. April and Billy were together last February, and Beck was born in late November. So it works on paper, but without the DNA test…" Her voice faded and she held her breath a moment, hating the flood of anxiety washing through her.

"You're not confident anymore?"

"Beck would be lucky to be a part of this family. You have a wonderful family."

"Billy told me the baby's momma died in a car accident."

Erika nodded. "Beck was in the car, but he survived. He didn't even have a scratch."

"A miracle."

Erika nodded again. "I think so, too."

"You've had him how long?"

"Three and a half weeks. Almost a month."

"What's your plan for him?"

"Find Beck's daddy and let his daddy take over."

"You don't want him?"

Erika exhaled hard. "I'm in no position to become a single mom. That is not the life I'd want for Beck. He deserves more than what I can give him."

"If Billy's not the father, what do you plan to do?"

"I'll keep looking."

"And if you can't find him?"

Emotion closed Erika's throat, knotting the words in her heart. Her heart wanted Beck to be with family, but her head questioned if she was the right family. Could she provide for a child when she sometimes struggled to provide for herself? Could she give Beck what he deserved in life? Growing up in her chaotic, alcohol-infused family she used to wish she had been adopted, wishing she had a more stable family to love her, and care for her.

Adoption wasn't a punishment. Adoption didn't mean Beck wasn't loved. It meant the opposite, that he was so valuable that Erika wanted him to have a family where he'd be raised with patience, and kindness, respect, and most of all love. Lots and lots of love, unlike April's childhood. And unlike her own. "I'd consider all options for him, including adoption."

Erika could feel Mrs. Wyatt's hard stare. She sensed she hadn't given Mrs. Wyatt the right answer but she wasn't going to lie to Billy's mother.

She glanced down at Beck and saw that he'd stopped sucking vigorously. His eyes were closing and the nipple just pressed against his mouth. She carefully eased the bottle from his lips, set the bottle on the table, and put Beck on her shoulder to gently burp him. He cuddled into the hollow of her shoulder and neck, his small fist pressed to her skin. She dipped her head, kissed the top of his head with its fine golden hair. There were only a few strands, so few that if you didn't look carefully he appeared bald, but Erika saw them, and she was delighted by them, as they were new in the past month. He was growing up, getting bigger every day.

Could she give him up for adoption?

Could she really hand him over to strangers?

The tightness returned to her chest, tightness and a panic she couldn't explain. She did love him, she'd come to love him, but did that give her the right to keep him? To raise him?

She looked up at Mrs. Wyatt who was still watching her.

"You're attached to him, aren't you?" the older woman asked.

"He's a wonderful baby," Erika said softly. "He deserves the sun and the moon and the stars."

"I think you and Billy need to do some talking. Some

real talking. When he comes back in, I'll keep Beck, and you two find somewhere private to speak."

Erika didn't need time alone with Billy. In her mind, there was nothing to discuss. They just needed him to do the test, and then they'd have the information they needed, but she didn't want to contradict Mrs. Wyatt, not when she'd been so welcoming to her. "I'd hate to leave Beck with you again as he might wake—"

"I've had four boys of my own, Erika. I can handle a baby for an hour or more."

Billy stepped into the den then, and glanced from his mother to Erika. "Did I just hear my name?"

"You did," his mother answered. "I was just telling Erika that when you have a minute, you and she should go somewhere private to talk."

"Joe's giving me a break. I was just going to make a sandwich and then I'm free for a bit."

"Good. Make your sandwich, and I'll keep an eye on Beck." Summer hesitated. "You'd probably have the most privacy in the barn. I don't think anyone's in there right now."

While Billy made his sandwich, Erika retrieved the car seat from upstairs and tucked Beck into it before placing it on the floor next to Mrs. Wyatt's feet.

She then bundled up and marched out to the barn with Billy, snow slipping inside her shoes, making her nose wrinkle.

Reaching the barn, Billy handed her half of his sandwich. "Here, you're probably hungry," he said, after closing the barn door behind them.

It was a huge ham and cheddar sandwich, with lots of honey mustard on thick homemade white bread. "I'm not that hungry," she answered.

"I'm not going to eat in front of you, so please, keep me company."

She took a small bite. It was good—the bread soft, the mustard tangy, the ham flavorful. "This is good," she said, taking another bite, but it was rather challenging separating the sandwich from the odiferous barn. The smell of animals, hay, and manure were potent. "But it's rather fragrant in here, isn't it?"

Billy lifted an eyebrow. "It's a barn."

"I've never been in one before."

"You've been to county fairs, haven't you?"

"To go on the rides and eat fair food."

"You didn't visit any of the animal exhibits?"

"I didn't even know there were animal exhibits."

"Are you that much of a city girl?"

"I grew up in Riverside, it's not a city, as in urban, but I wasn't surrounded by farms, either."

He'd finished his sandwich and he wiped his hand on the seat of his jeans. He had lean hips, a tight small butt which his tight Wranglers showed off to perfection. She watched him walk between the horse stalls. Horses nickered at him, and he stopped to give attention to several.

"Do you have your horses in here?" she asked.

"Yes. Notorious," he said, gesturing to a dark brown horse, "and Val," he added, pointing to a brown and white horse.

"Val?"

"Valentine," he answered. "That mark around his eye looks like a heart."

"That's cute."

Billy gave her a look that made her insides squirm.

"Sweet?" she said instead.

He gave her another long look.

Erika grimaced. "I'm sorry. I don't know anything about horses." She hesitated then said, "And I owe you an apology."

"You do?"

"I shouldn't have come here. I should have waited to track you down at a different venue. I'm sorry for dropping in like this, and involving your whole family. I did exactly what you didn't want to happen—"

"You don't want April's son?"

Her mouth opened, closed.

"Mom said you're considering adoption if you can't find his father."

"It's one of the options under consideration."

"Why wouldn't you keep him?"

"I can barely take care of myself sometimes. I don't know

how I'd take care of him, too."

He studied her for a long time, blue gaze assessing. "I'll take a test tomorrow. I imagine it will take a few days to get results."

"Thank you."

"But if he's not mine…"

That ache was back in her chest, and she opened her mouth to speak, but no sound came out. "As you said, that's a bridge to cross later."

Chapter Three

BILLY WASN'T COMFORTABLE with the direction the conversation had turned. "What would you do?"

"I'd do what I thought was best for Beck. I'd consider all options. Including adoption."

His gut cramped. The idea of a baby being given up, given away, didn't sit right with him. Children weren't disposable, and family was meant to take care of family. "I can't believe you're really serious. I thought it was a test for me, a way to gauge my commitment."

Erika's cheeks flushed and she looked away. "You make me sound heartless."

He'd always thought she was pretty, and he'd always worked hard to ignore it because she was April's cousin, and she didn't strike him as the type of woman interested in just a good time, and those were the women he pursued. Far better to play with those who knew, and understood, the rules of the game.

But in this moment, Erika looked not just pretty, she looked vulnerable, and it woke a protective instinct in him. "Would never dream of calling you heartless. I am sure you've been doing your best to keep your head above water, being thrust into the role of guardian out of the blue."

She shot him a grateful look, which only served to strengthen his desire to not come at her when she was down. "It has been hard," she admitted. "I've been his sole caretaker for close to four weeks. I'd never cared for a baby before and had to learn everything, even as I made arrangements for April's cremation, and then moved her out of her apartment and made arrangements for all her things—" She broke off, drew a deep, unsteady breath. Her eyes, blue green shimmered turquoise with tears. "I reached out to April's mother, and she hung up on me. My mom and I haven't spoken in years. There is no one else in my family to go to. They'd already rejected April and the baby, and maybe that's a good thing because there will be no battle for custody—"

"Why doesn't your family want him?"

"It's not just him. They don't want me, either."

He heard the crack in her voice and the underlying pain. "Why?"

She brushed the tears away. "I hate crying," she muttered fiercely, pushing off the column to pace the floor. "Tears are so stupid."

He checked his smile. "I won't tell anyone, if that helps."

She lifted her head, giving him a crooked smile. "Don't make me laugh. I'm in a bad mood."

Billy bit down to keep from laughing. Even then he smiled. "Why doesn't your family want you?"

"I don't come from a family like yours. We didn't have a lot of love. I wasn't raised with hugs and laughter. I'm not confident in my parental skills. I can't help but think that there might be a truly wonderful family out there, desperate for a child—"

"You'd miss him."

"I would, yes. Absolutely. But at the same time, if I thought he was with people who would love him and provide for him? Be there for him throughout his life? Then I'd be happy, for him. I would." She stopped pacing to face him. "Have I ever told you what I do? What I'm studying?"

"You're a researcher?"

"No. A student." She dragged her hand over her head, pulling little blonde wisps from her loose ponytail. "I'm just a student. If I'd finished my degree, if I'd finished my dissertation and had a real job, and income, it'd all be different. But I'm not even halfway through."

"What is a dissertation?"

"It's a research project that completes the final step of my doctoral program, a compilation of academic and practical knowledge—"

"Doctoral?" he interrupted.

"I'm working toward my PhD in psychology."

He was impressed. But also completely ignorant about everything she was saying, making him feel as if he was in a foreign country listening to people speak a language he didn't know. "You're nearing the end of your degree?"

"The dissertation is all that's left, but it's a big chunk of the degree, and I haven't gotten anything done for the past month."

"When is it due?"

"It's not black and white like that. It's due when it's done, meaning when I've completed the research and writing. Most of my practical research is done. Now I need to structure and write it."

"How long does it take to write it?"

"Again, depends. I've been warned that it could take anywhere from fourteen months to twenty months." She grimaced. "I'm proving to be closer to the latter because I take on part-time jobs to help pay bills. I just finished a house sitting/dog sitting job when I got the call about Beck. Thank goodness, too. It would have been hard reaching JoJo's owner in Patagonia."

"JoJo?"

"A Chihuahua that likes to bite people." Her nose wrinkled. "Not a good fit with a baby."

"Uh, not a good fit with anyone."

She laughed, the sound light and surprisingly bright, almost joyful. "JoJo tolerated me toward the end. But the beginning was rough. Once I realized treats were the way to get her to stop snapping, I carried them in my pocket all the time. Wouldn't be in the same room with her without them."

"This is why I like big dogs."

"Oh, and big dogs don't bite? Come on."

"No dog should ever bite."

"You have two very big dogs here."

"We used to have three, but we lost our big boy, Runt, just after Christmas. Granddad took it really hard. Runt was his boy."

"I'm sorry."

Billy realized yet again he'd misjudged her. April and Erika were nothing alike, and that was both good and bad. Good, because Erika obviously had her act together, and was someone who could be counted on to make the right decisions for Beck. Bad because Erika intrigued Billy, and he couldn't remember the last time a woman interested him at any level other than sexual. Erika was beautiful, but she was also smart, and he liked talking to her. He wanted to keep talking to her and that was not his norm.

"I don't know how your family could not want you," he said abruptly. "You're incredibly successful—"

"But not a member of their church." She gave him a tight, bright smile but he could see it didn't reach her eyes. "And if you don't believe, and don't follow their principles, well, you don't matter. You're a heathen, and an outsider."

"Ouch."

"Yeah, ouch." She glanced toward the house, expression troubled. "But it is what it is. Dysfunction perpetuates dysfunction." Her shoulders slumped and she looked weary. "It's why I wanted to study psychology, why I wanted to learn, and grow, and try to learn what healthy behavior is. I don't want to be like my family—"

"I don't think you're anything like your family."

"You don't know that."

"As soon as you heard about April, you headed to Las Vegas and jumped into action, taking on her son"—he broke off, correcting himself—"possibly my son. You put your life on hold to handle her affairs and try to find Beck's father. That's admirable—"

"But it shouldn't be admirable! It should just be what people do for each other. It should just be decency—"

"*Exactly.*" The conviction in her voice did something to him, making his chest tighten. He liked her. She wasn't the enemy. And she wasn't the problem. "I'll get the paternity test done in Bozeman tomorrow. We should have results soon after, I imagine."

"Thank you." She drew a deep breath and squared her shoulders. "I'm thinking I should retrieve Beck from your mom. I don't want to take advantage of her kindness."

"She wouldn't have offered if she didn't want to do it. Mom is no pushover."

Erika hesitated. "Do you mind telling me why she needs the walker? Is it arthritis?"

"We used to think it was arthritis, but she was recently diagnosed with MS. Fortunately, she's on new medicine and it's really helped her. Just two years ago Joe was carrying her up and down the stairs."

"Thank goodness for new medicines."

"Agreed."

BACK IN THE house, Erika changed Beck's diapers, and then after giving him a bottle, walked him around, including a look at all the framed family photos in the hall, that also went up the stairs. Baby photos and family photos. Faded color photos of boys in football uniforms, as well as team wrestling photos. There were other photos of showing animals, and early rodeo wins. A photo of Christmas that had to be back from the seventies by the collared shirts the guys were wearing.

Granddad joined her in the hall. "Those are my boys," he said gruffly, pointing to two handsome teenagers holding trophies in a rodeo arena. "JC and Samuel. Their first national win in team roping before they were invited to join the professional association."

She glanced at Melvin, heart tender. "How old were they there?"

"JC would have been about nineteen. Sam seventeen."

"They were good."

"They were good boys." Melvin's voice deepened. "Did everything together. A lot like Billy and Tommy. Best friends."

She searched Melvin's strong features, his skin weathered from years outdoors. In her research on the Wyatts, she'd read how Melvin's sons had died together in an accident when they were in their late twenties. JC and Summer already had four little boys. Sam hadn't yet married, but had been seeing someone for a while. "It must have been devastating," she said softly.

"Hard losing them both like that, yes." He reached out and ran his hand lightly across the top of Beck's head. "But they went to be with my Bess, and hopefully they're in a better place."

"And then you raised JC's boys."

"Family first always."

Again her heart ached, and she had to hold her breath, to keep emotion in check. "They're lucky to have you."

"They saved me. Without them, I doubt I'd still be here. They gave me purpose. They kept me busy. They gave me a lot of love." He looked down at her, with the same blue eyes Billy had, with the same blue eyes Beck had. "At the end of the day, love is what matters. Integrity, honesty, respect… those all matter, but they mean nothing without love."

For the second time that day Erika was on the verge of tears, and she didn't want to cry. She didn't like feeling so emotional. "I hope Beck is your great-grandson, if only that he could have you for a great-grandfather. He'd be so lucky to be part of this family."

"Well, if he is, you are, too. We'd be family together."

Dinner that night was less rowdy than the night before. Sam and Ivy were missing, and Joe and Sophie were eating dinner together at their place. Tommy had made dinner, his favorite, fried chicken with mashed potatoes, and Erika silently marveled that the Wyatt men all seemed to cook. She didn't say this, of course, since her own culinary skill was next to nothing, but she admired Summer for making sure her sons knew how to fend for themselves.

It was during dessert, over coffee and leftover birthday cake, that Tommy brought up Erika's studies. "Billy said you were in graduate school, working on your PhD. That's pretty impressive."

She blushed as all attention shifted to her. "It's been a commitment."

"What drew you to psychology?"

"I liked the idea of helping people. It's an interesting field."

"How much more do you have left?" Summer asked.

"I'm in the writing phase of my dissertation. All the research is done."

"I don't really know what that entails," Melvin said, "but I suspect it means you spend a lot of time at a computer."

Erika smiled at him. "That's exactly what it entails. Lots of drafting, lots of rewriting, lots of double-checking my research, sometimes finding huge holes in my work."

Summer was listening intently. "That can't be easy when you're caring for a baby on your own."

"It's not," Erika admitted. "I haven't done anything in the past month. I'm trying not to panic, but I'm behind."

"I hate that feeling," Tommy said, leaning forward to take another sliver of cake. "I don't like being behind. Makes me irritable."

"Makes you an ass," Billy corrected. "But that's also what makes you such a good competitor. You never say die."

"You can't," Tommy agreed, licking the frosting from his fork prongs. "Wyatts never quit, and we never give up." He looked up, a dimple flashing in his cheek. "Even when we should."

"So, what's next?" Melvin asked her.

"I'm trying not to get anxious, but I do need to get back to work soon. I need to graduate on time. I need to start earning money—and to do that I need my degree, need work, need to become a licensed therapist."

"We could use a therapist in the family," Tommy said. "Billy could use a lot of help, someone to help him sort through his fear of relationships. Why does love scare him—"

"Alright, that's enough," Billy interrupted, no more laughter in his voice. "I'm not interested in being dissected—"

"You mean analyzed," Tommy corrected.

"Same thing." Billy pushed back from the table, and began collecting the dessert plates and coffee cups. "I'm making it an early night tonight," he said. "Tomorrow I'm back on the road."

Erika hadn't thought she'd see any more of Billy that night, but he knocked on her bedroom door after she and Beck had retired for the evening. She opened the door, pointed to the baby sleeping in the portable crib, and then stepped out of her room, closing the door behind her.

"You okay?" she asked.

His brow creased. "Why wouldn't I be?"

"Tommy just seemed to take a dig or two at you."

Billy shrugged. "That's normal."

"But it seemed to be a little too personal, especially when it came to you and relationships."

"That I don't do relationships?" His big shoulders shifted, and his flannel shirt, already half unbuttoned, fell open, exposing a lot of skin. And muscles. Impressive muscles. "It's true. Not something I try to hide."

She studied him intently, aware that there was more behind his breezy tone. "Maybe that's why April didn't reach out to you after she discovered she was pregnant. Maybe she knew you didn't do relationships so the whole parenthood thing was a moot point."

"If that was the case, she shouldn't have assumed."

"Maybe it was hard for her. She clearly had feelings for you—"

"No."

"*Yes.* She spent a lot of time chasing you from rodeo to rodeo. She made a whole photo album about one of your special weekends. You don't commemorate a one-night stand with a photo album. You forget a one-night stand. You put the man, and the memory, away. But she didn't do that. She wanted to remember you. She... cherished you."

"I made no promises to her. There were no commitments. Your cousin was an adult. A consenting adult who enjoyed sex. I enjoyed sex. We enjoyed sex together. Not sure why that gives you the right to subject me to your psychoanalysis babble."

"Just because you don't understand it, doesn't mean it's babble."

"Just because I didn't graduate with a plethora of college degrees doesn't mean I'm a hick."

"I never said that."

"But you have formed strong opinions about me, and I'm not sure they're all justified."

"Everyone forms opinions. It's human nature."

"Want to know my opinion of you?"

She stiffened even as her gaze met his. "Not if you're going to be unkind."

"Why do you think I'd be unkind?"

"You're not a fan of psychology."

"I think you truly want to help people, and I respect that. But April wasn't a saint, and she may have fantasized about a future with me, but that wasn't ever going to happen. Did she keep Beck from me on purpose? I don't know. Was she not sure Beck was mine? I don't know that, either. All I know is that you're here with him, and tomorrow I'll take a DNA test, and soon we'll have facts. Facts are what matter now. The rest of it… doesn't really matter, does it?"

"I think you're better at compartmentalizing than I am. It's something I need to work on."

"You seem to think you need a lot of work. I don't see it."

She looked away, averting her face. "We can always be better."

"We can always torture ourselves about our weaknesses, too. That doesn't interest me, though. I'd rather get stuff done than spend my life beating myself up."

※

BILLY STUDIED HER delicate profile, her elegant features framed by a mass of golden hair. Erika did little to her appearance. He couldn't even see any makeup, other than maybe a touch of mascara that she hadn't yet taken off, and even without makeup, she was beautiful. Naturally pretty. In any other situation he'd be flirting with her, teasing her, testing her response to him, but this wasn't a normal situation. He wasn't going to take her to bed. For one, she was Beck's guardian. For another, she was April's cousin—which was a whole thing in and of itself.

He liked women. Enjoyed bedding them. But he didn't just hook up with anyone. It had to make sense. He had rules. No married women. No engaged women. No women seeing someone seriously.

No chicks with kids.

No pretending he was looking for love.

No pretending there was a chance for a relationship.

He didn't want a wife. He didn't want children. He just wanted to be free and pursue his career. It was what he cared about, and what he wanted most.

But with Erika just an arm's length away, he felt aware of her as a woman, a warm, achingly beautiful woman, as well as a woman who had no interest in him, and God help him, but that appealed. He loved challenges, responded to them, but this wasn't a challenge he could accept. So he wouldn't make a move, but that didn't make her any less physically appealing.

If anything, it made her more so.

"After the DNA test tomorrow, I'm going to be heading on to Boise. I need to be there a few days early as one of my sponsors has a VIP party for me to attend Thursday night, and then a meet and greet at the local mall Friday at noon."

Erika's brow creased. "So what do we do while we wait for the test results? Stay in Bozeman? Follow you to Idaho?"

"You could come to Idaho, or you could head home and I'll call you once we have the results."

She looked uncertain. "You think I should drive all the way back to Southern California?"

"If you're tired of being on the road. I like it. But I'm not the one traveling with a baby." He spotted Tommy from the corner of his eye, coming up the stairs. He gave him a don't-bother-us look, and Tommy continued on to the room they shared. "If the test says I'm Beck's dad, I'll come get him."

"Before your next rodeo weekend?"

His gaze narrowed. "I don't know if it'd be that soon. My schedule is pretty structured. I'd need to figure out logistics."

"Kind of like me and my studies."

She had a point and he shrugged. "Don't go home then. Follow me to Boise. We'll get you a motel room not far from the rodeo grounds. You and Beck can stay there while we sort out the rest."

"And if he is your son? What will you do then?"

"Figure out how to manage a baby while living on the road."

"You're going to take him with you?" she asked incredulously. "From rodeo to rodeo?"

He heard her tone, but it didn't bother him. The only thing that would bother him would be abandoning a child he'd made. And he wasn't going to do that. But he also needed to compete. It was how he made money, and he could make amazing money, if he returned to the National Finals in Las Vegas next December, but to do that, he had to do well all year long. If he missed too many events, and failed to place in money at events, then he wouldn't qualify. He couldn't let that happen. "I'd probably have to hire a sitter. I'm sure I could find someone—"

"A stranger," she interrupted.

"It's a job. People do it all the time."

"He needs to be with people he knows. He needs stability, security, consistency."

"Then come with us. If I have to pay a sitter, I might as well pay you."

Her jaw dropped. "Travel with you from rodeo to rodeo?"

"Lots of families do it. The rig is really a trailer, and it's quite comfortable with a kitchen, bathroom, bedroom—"

"I'd never live in a trailer with you."

"I could get you a motel room in each town. I wouldn't put you somewhere too cheap. I'd want you and Beck safe."

"While you'd stay in the rig, on your own," she said.

He lifted a brow. "You want me to sleep in the motel with you every night instead?"

"*No.*"

"Then what? What are you objecting to?"

"Being on the road with an infant! Traveling from town to town for months on end."

"That's what I do, darlin'."

"A rodeo cowboy."

"That's who I am."

"Forever?"

"Certainly for as long as I can."

"What about Beck?"

"What about him?"

"How are you going to manage it? Traveling, competing, taking care of a baby?"

"I can't, not on my own. But with your help, I can make it work, and with my help, you can sock away some money and still earn your degree."

When she said nothing, he added quietly, "We also don't need to have this conversation until we have the test results back—"

"Everyone else in this family seems sure he's yours."

"Then once we have those results, you can leave him, and his bag, and his car seat with me, and you'll be able to return to Riverside and your life there."

Her head jerked up, her gaze locking with his. She looked worried, but something else. Scared. Sad.

Why sad?

And then he understood. She'd become attached to Beck. She didn't want to just abandon Beck. He respected her for that. "You know, you aren't responsible for him anymore. You have no legal obligation—"

"No legal obligation, but just a moral one. He's a baby. He needs love. I'm not sure you know how to care for a baby—"

"Or give love?" he finished silkily.

He watched, fascinated, as pink washed through her cheeks.

"You obviously come from a close-knit family," she stammered. "It's clear you love your brothers, your mother, your grandfather, but you've had a lifetime to form that bond. You don't have a bond with Beck yet, and babies require a lot of patience, tenderness, and self-sacrifice. I'd find it very hard to just leave Beck here and drive away and feel okay about it. I would worry about him all the time. I would worry that maybe," she looked away, her voice cracking, "he'd be confused. I wouldn't want him to miss me. Nor would I want him to ever think I just abandoned him."

"Maybe we just slow down and take this step by step. First the test, and then the results. Let's not think about anything beyond that. Just test. And then just the results. We can do that, can't we?"

She nodded.

"Good." He gave her a faint, wry smile. "So can I. Try to get some sleep. I think we both could use it tonight."

Chapter Four

He was on the road, on the outskirts of Boise when the call came. He'd been warned that morning in Bozeman, that even with a rush fee, it could be twenty-four hours before the results came in but they'd do their best. The DNA results had come back sooner, and he was a 99 percent match. There was no question that he was Beck's biological father.

Call over, Billy focused on the road, but his thoughts weren't on the ribbon of black asphalt stretching before him. His thoughts were of Beck in Erika's car, and how he wasn't just a baby, but his.

It was that simple, and that difficult. He was a dad now, and he'd be a dad… forever.

Billy exhaled slowly, running a hand over his bristled jaw. That call changed everything, and emotions rolled through him, thoughts tangled.

He'd had a son for all these months and he didn't know. Billy wondered if April was ever going to tell him. Had she planned on just surprising him one day, showing up at the rodeo with the baby, much like Erika had?

He wished he'd known what April had been thinking, wished he'd known she was pregnant. She should have told him. She should have reached out the moment she knew. No, they weren't planning on seeing more of each other, but pregnancy was different. Pregnancy wasn't about romance or sex, it was about life. Their child's life. And maybe he'd been a little too blunt when he'd told her that he didn't see a future for them, and that he thought maybe it was time they stepped back, focused on other people, but how else were you supposed to end things with someone? Ignore them? Ghost them? That wasn't his style. Far better to be honest. Aboveboard. And he'd never been unkind. But he had let her know he was moving on, and he was asking her to move on, too. Leave him alone. Focus on her life. Which might just be why she didn't tell him about the pregnancy. He hoped it was because she was confused, not spiteful. Because keeping his son from him wasn't right. He would have wanted to know as soon as April suspected she was pregnant. He would have wanted to be part of Beck's life from the beginning.

Twenty minutes later, he signaled that they were taking the exit off the freeway. He checked his rearview mirror to see if Erika was paying attention, and she was, following his truck and trailer off the highway and down along a frontage road, and then down another road until he pulled in at a motel, and parked in a spot on the side where his long white trailer could fit without being in anyone's way.

While Erika stretched her legs, Billy checked her in, using his credit card to pay for the room, and then carried all of the baby's things in to the room at the end of the hall on the ground floor. The room had a little patio with a view of the parking lot and Billy's trailer. "I'm going to find food," he said. "Do what you need to do. I should be back soon."

"Take the key," she said. "Just in case I'm in the shower."

Billy tried not to dwell on the image in his head of her in the shower. He didn't want to picture her naked. Didn't need physical desire to complicate things more than they already were. By the time he returned, she was sitting on the bed, giving Beck a bottle. Beck was in his jammies, and she was in comfortable sweats, her long hair wet, her face scrubbed clean.

"Success," he said, placing the paper bag filled with chicken sandwiches between them. "Three for me, two for you. No fries. Trying to be good."

Erika laughed. "You have an interesting definition of being good."

"Fries are fattening."

"And breaded chicken isn't?"

"I like my chicken crispy. None of that pitiful grilled breasts for me." He dropped into a chair, and extended his legs. "I'm hungry," he said, tucking into the first sandwich.

They ate in silence, the only sound besides crinkled foil wrappers was Beck greedily sucking on his bottle.

Billy watched Beck work his bottle, his little brow wrinkled with concentration.

His baby. His kid.

Crazy.

Amazing.

Amazing that Erika had figured it out.

He waited until she'd finished a sandwich to let her know that the DNA results had come in, and that they'd confirmed what she'd said—Beck was his.

For a long minute Erika said nothing. "Are you surprised?"

He gathered the crumpled paper bags and foil wrappers. "Not really, no," he said, tossing them into the motel's waste basket.

"But you fought the truth—"

"I didn't fight anything. I just needed time to come to terms with the fact that I had a baby. A baby who'd been alive for months without me ever knowing anything about him."

She put Beck up on her shoulder and began burping him. "It sounds as if you're turning things around. Blaming April."

He arched a brow. "You don't think she should have told me?"

"Maybe she did. Maybe she wrote to you, or called, or sent you a message through Instagram. Maybe you ignored her—"

"I didn't."

"Maybe you'd blocked her."

Yes, he *had* blocked her. On his phone and on Instagram. She wouldn't stop sending him selfies of her naked. Titty pics. Bikini waxed privates. It was uncomfortable, especially once he was seeing other women and she wasn't taking no for an answer. "There were other ways she could have reached me, especially if she wanted to tell me about the pregnancy. She just needed to say there was a baby—"

"And you would have believed her?"

His jaw ground tight. Erika saw far more than he'd like her to see. "Probably not without a paternity test, no."

"What did she do to make you so mistrust her?"

"You weren't in touch with her for the past few years. You yourself said you'd lost touch with her. I don't want to be unkind, but the April I knew wasn't the April you remember. The April I knew craved attention, and would do anything for attention, and not just from me, but from a number of guys."

Erika looked at him for a long moment, expression guarded. "Why weren't you surprised that Beck was yours when the test results came in? What changed your mind?"

He hesitated a long moment. "Mom had said he looks just like me. She said she knew he was a Wyatt the moment she met him." Billy shifted in the chair, propping one boot over the other. "Mom doesn't tend to exaggerate about things like that."

"You never told me."

"I wanted my proof. I'm a hard facts guy, and I needed

the paternity results to confirm everyone's suspicions. This is one of those things you need to test, prove." He shrugged, shoulders shifting. "Which I now have."

"And the test results change everything. Right?"

"I wouldn't say they change everything, but things will be different."

"How?"

"I'm Beck's father."

"Okay. So you'll settle down and raise him? You'll stop putting your life in danger—"

"My life isn't in danger."

"Every time you compete, you're risking your life."

"Gross exaggeration."

"I've read the statistics. The rodeo is dangerous."

"Life is dangerous. I could get hurt in a car accident just as easily. Look at April—"

"Yes, look at April. She's gone. Do we really need you gone, too?"

"Can you not jinx me? I try to avoid negative thoughts like that."

"It's called being mature and facing reality."

He rose and scooped up his hat off the round table. "Well, I don't like your reality. It's pretty bleak, if you ask me."

❦

ERIKA WINCED AS Billy left, closing the door firmly behind

him. After he'd gone, she stared at the door a long moment, unsure of how she felt. On one hand she was elated that she'd been right. Billy Wyatt was Beck's dad. But on the other, she was troubled that April hadn't ever told Billy. She'd had nine months of pregnancy to let Billy know, and even if Billy had blocked her number, April wouldn't have found it difficult to track him down. Erika didn't know him and she'd still managed to find him, in three different places, three different weekends.

She rose from the bed, locked the door, and closed the curtains at the window, aware that in the end, what April did, or didn't do, wasn't important anymore. April wasn't here. But Beck was, and Billy was, and father and son were finally together, the way they were supposed to be.

❦

Erika had gone to bed feeling almost euphoric. She'd united a father and son and she'd be able to start getting caught up with her work. Billy would be able to take Beck for a good part of each day, giving her time for some undisturbed writing. The great thing about a laptop was that she could work almost anywhere, including a small motel room off the freeway.

Unfortunately, the next morning Billy got a call that Tommy's truck broke down a couple hours east of Idaho Falls, and Billy was needed to collect Tommy's trailer with the horses while Tommy had his truck towed to an auto shop. But instead of returning to Boise that night, Billy stayed with Tommy in Idaho Falls, and it was late Wednesday before they arrived in town, with Tommy's truck still in the shop, waiting on a part from Salt Lake City.

Wednesday Billy wasn't available because the body shop called and the part had come in and Tommy would be able to pick up his truck later that day, so Billy and Tommy planned to return to Idaho Falls after they worked out their horses and did some training. The brothers dropped by the motel on their way out of town, spending fifteen minutes playing with Beck before they climbed back in Billy's truck.

Erika wouldn't say she fumed as they drove away from the motel, but she was definitely anxious, and frustrated. She'd really wanted to get some solid work done this week, and so far, nothing. Beck wasn't helping matters by deciding he wouldn't nap for longer than thirty-minute stretches meant she couldn't get anything done. She knew Billy had an appearance or something tomorrow, but surely there'd be some time in there where he could take care of Beck so she could focus for three or four hours.

But Thursday was just like the rest of the week, and Billy had sponsors who wanted to take him to breakfast and then he'd been invited to a local Rotary lunch where he'd been asked to say a few words to the group, thanking them for their support to the local charity all these years, a charity that Billy cared about, too. Thursday afternoon he needed to exercise his horses. Thursday evening he had an event to attend.

Friday he managed to squeeze in breakfast with Beck before he had to show up for Boise's annual rodeo parade. He had an autograph session and another VIP something and then the rodeo itself that night, followed by a party after. She didn't go to the Friday night rodeo. It was too late for Beck and she was too annoyed by Billy's sense of self-importance. If every week was like this week, when would he have time for his son?

When would she get anything she needed done?

But Saturday morning arrived, and the sky was a gorgeous clear blue, and the sun shone brightly and Erika woke up feeling hopeful, optimistic despite the challenging week. Since the rodeo was a day event today, she also thought maybe she and Beck should go. She'd finally see her first rodeo, and perhaps she'd have a better idea of just what it was that Billy did.

She sent Billy a text that she and Beck would be heading to the rodeo grounds, and he replied that he'd left a ticket for her at Will Call.

Erika left the car seat in the car, strapping Beck into the baby carrier instead. She adjusted him in the carrier, making sure he was comfortably seated and strapped in, before locking the car and heading toward the entrance. Like Tucson, people were dressed up in western wear, denim and leather-fringed coats, jeans and boots, and of course lots of cowboy hats from expensive-looking felt Stetsons to the straw kind that looked as if they'd be found on a beach in Cancun.

Her ticket was waiting for her as promised, and she and Beck entered the grounds, and then bought a program because it seemed like the right thing to do. It would be Beck's first souvenir of his dad's career and Erika looked forward to leafing through it, too.

Her phone vibrated in her pocket and she pulled it out and checked the text message. Billy wanted her to come and say hello when she arrived. He told her to walk to the back where the livestock was and he'd be on the lookout for her.

She texted that she was on her way now, and she made her way through the throng to the pens with the horses and bulls. She eyed a big red bull warily. He gave her an equally unfriendly look.

She spotted Billy before he saw her. He was talking to a pretty cowgirl in skintight jeans, flashy white fringed chaps, and a snug turquoise western blouse. Her hat was the same color as her chaps and her long blonde hair hung in feminine ringlets down her back. The cowgirl was laughing a lot as she batted her thick false eyelashes at Billy. Apparently he was hilarious. Erika rolled her eyes, thinking he wasn't that funny. But girls and women loved him. They couldn't seem to get enough.

Billy saw Erika then and gave her a faint nod.

She tried to smash her irritation. She shouldn't let his popularity bother her. She wasn't interested in him. And she shouldn't judge him. It wasn't a good thing to do… with anyone.

She didn't know what Billy said to the cowgirl, but the girl gave him a light pat on the chest and moved away, but not without shooting Erika a curious look. Her expression changed when she saw the baby. Erika didn't know if she should feel vindicated or not.

"Glad you made it," he said, reaching out to adjust the knit cap on Beck's head. "Have any trouble getting in?"

"No." Erika glanced at the back of the flashy cowgirl. "Is that woman a barrel racer?"

He followed her gaze, shook his head. "No. She's part of Boise's equestrian drill team."

She arched a brow.

"Like flag girls without a flag. They perform choreographed routines on horses."

"I've entered a world I knew nothing about."

"And for your information, Lily was asking about Sam. She had a soft spot for him. I broke the news that he's married now. No longer on the market."

Erika shrugged carelessly. "I wasn't worried."

"You looked jealous."

"I looked jealous?" She made a soft scoffing sound. "Not at all. Who you see, and what you do, is none of my business." She glanced down at Beck who was squirming against her, his small feet reminding her that she needed to use a restroom soon. "I should find a restroom before I sit down.

Do you know where any are?"

"There are portable toilets everywhere, and then some regular bathrooms under the stands. They'll probably have long lines, so just be prepared."

She dreaded taking Beck into a dirty bathroom, let alone a porta-potty. "Would you mind holding him for me while I go? Hopefully it won't take too long, especially if I use one of the porta-potties."

"My first event is coming up soon. I need to get ready."

"You really don't have ten minutes?"

"I wish I did. But I need to warm up and stretch, get focused—"

"You're serious?"

"You could use the bathroom in my rig if you want. It's a bit of a walk, but you'd have privacy and a clean place to put Beck."

All week long she'd waited for him to step up and help out. All week she waited for him to think of her, and what she needed to do. All week, she'd tried to be patient, telling herself he'd eventually be there for her, but no, not once. It was only ever about him.

"So that's a no," she said quietly, flatly.

"Erika, my entire event lasts eight seconds. It's a hard eight seconds. I've got to prepare—"

"You're always going to have an excuse."

"What does that mean?"

She'd heard how his voice dropped, a hard edge to his

words, but she was too frustrated to care. "It means you will always come first—"

"Sorry, sweetheart, but this is my job. When I'm at work, work comes first."

She was already angry, but when he called her sweetheart, in that condescending, insulting tone, talking to her as if she was stupid, a goodtime girl who needed to be put in her place, she just saw red. "You're the big man. Gosh, it must feel good to be you."

"You're sure you want to be a therapist? Do you hear how you talk to people?"

"I'm not counseling you."

"Perfect, because I didn't ask for your input, nor do I need it."

Her heart raced. Blood roared in her ears. "I haven't been able to work in weeks. I haven't had a chance to do anything for myself this week. And you'd said my work was important, too—"

"It is. But the weekends are mine. They're when I work."

"No, hotshot. The weekends are when I work, too. Or at least, when I'm supposed to work."

"I don't know what to say. I don't have time for this. I need to go."

"And what am I supposed to do?"

"Whatever you want to do. You've got your own car here, you can go back to the motel, and wait for the day to end. Or, you could sit in the stands, watch the rodeo." He paused, flashed a smile that wasn't particularly friendly. "Cheer me on."

"You have responsibilities, Billy Wyatt."

"And apparently so do you."

※

ERIKA FUMED AS she drove back to the motel, thinking the last thing she wanted to do was sit in the stands and watch grown men ride and rope and do whatever else they did. Even though she'd been raised in Clovis, California, she wasn't a fan of rodeos, and didn't love anything about cowboy culture. She couldn't even imagine how competing in small rodeos across the country could pay bills. It didn't seem remotely like a real job.

Erika's parents had been firmly middle class. They'd owned their own business in downtown Riverside, an escrow company her mom helped manage with her dad. Erika held numerous jobs throughout high school, something that proved essential when her parents divorced her senior year after discovering her mother—of all people—had been having an affair. The divorce was acrimonious and protracted and by the time they'd sold the business Erika's freshman year of college, there wasn't much left after all the legal fees. Her mother moved with her new love to a beach community in Oregon, and her father moved to Atlanta, wanting to get as far away from the West Coast as possible—which turned out to mean, getting away from her as well.

Arriving back at the motel, Erika discovered housekeeping was in her room, and she took the baby carrier and diaper bag to the motel's reception where she could find a discrete corner to sit and give Beck a bottle. The middle-aged woman at the reception desk was cheerful and talkative, asking Erika about Beck's age and commenting on how he seemed like a really good baby.

Erika flashed a quick smile as she lifted Beck from his car seat and sat him up on her lap. She could feel his wet diaper and needed to change him, but would wait until she was back in her room. "He is a good baby," she agreed, fixing his bottle next. "As long as you keep his tummy full, he's a happy guy."

"Typical man," the motel receptionist retorted.

Erika smiled and popped the bottle's nipple into the baby's mouth. "Are you from Boise?" she asked, just being conversational.

"Born and raised," the woman said proudly.

"This is my first time here. Beautiful area. Love the mountains."

"Here for the rodeo?"

Erika wasn't sure how to answer that. Finally, she said, "I've a friend in town."

"Well, if you've got time, check out the rodeo. It's a lot of fun. There should be some bleacher seats open. I'm heading over as soon as I get off work."

"I don't know much about the rodeo," Erika confessed,

and that much was true. She'd never actually watched one, although she'd come close today, but Billy had made her so angry that she wasn't going to sit there and watch him, not after he'd been something of a jerk.

"I'm a fan. I go every year." The woman leaned across the counter. "Some of those boys are good-looking. In fact, some of the families and friends stay here. You'll see them pulling in later. You can recognize them by their hats and boots."

April came to mind. April in the photo book, naked save a cowboy hat. Suddenly Erika wanted to be anywhere but sitting here. She put Beck back in his car seat, clicked the straps into place and lifted the seat and diaper bag. "I'm sure my room is ready by now," she said. "Thanks for letting me hang out here for a bit."

"Thanks for the company. Don't forget to check out the rodeo later. You'll be glad you did."

The sun and excitement must have worn Beck out because once they were back in the cool motel room, and Erika had drawn the blackout curtains, Beck fell asleep and slept for hours.

Erika told herself this would be the perfect time to work, but she was too upset. Too frazzled. Too frustrated.

She flopped on the queen-size bed and tried to nap herself, but she couldn't relax, her brain spinning this way and that.

She hated being mad. She hated that awful hot almost

out of control feeling she felt when her temper flared. She'd never given in to outbursts when growing up—she wasn't allowed the luxury—and she'd learned to bottle everything inside. But as she grew up, and learned to live independently, she'd begun trying to deal with her emotions instead of just smashing them down and going numb.

She wasn't numb now. She felt emotional and angry and incredibly confused.

She'd been adamant about uniting Beck with his father. She'd also been adamant that she wasn't going to get attached to Beck. She wasn't looking to be a single mom. She wasn't looking to be a mom, not for years, not until she'd met other goals, and they were goals that had to be accomplished in the proper order.

Graduate degree.

Work.

Build career, build financial security.

Date.

Meet someone solid and trustworthy.

Have a long engagement, develop relationship.

Get married.

Spend a few years as a couple, focusing on marriage.

Then get pregnant and start a family.

There were steps to be taken, steps that would ensure she wasn't making a mistake, or rushing into anything.

Because school had been her number one priority, Erika hadn't been dating. Her last 'boyfriend' had been almost three years ago, and her last date fourteen months ago, and that date, tepid and uninspiring, made her realize she'd rather be alone than with someone who bored her. And so she wrote off men and dating until she'd accomplished more of her goals, and she'd been focused exclusively on her goals until April died and she got the call that she was April's backup plan for Beck.

For the past month Erika's goals, those goals she'd carefully nurtured, had been shoved to a back burner, but she couldn't leave her goals there.

She couldn't leave herself on the back burner.

If she had the means, if she thought she could support Beck, she'd pack him up and head back home right now. She'd let Billy find her and come up with a parenting plan that made sense, but until then, she'd take care of Beck the way she always had—with love and patience.

Even if she hadn't become attached to Beck, she still wouldn't like the thought of him living in a trailer, traveling from rodeo to rodeo. That was no life for a baby.

If Billy settled down, if he took a job, for example, on a ranch like the Wyatt ranch, or even better, settled down in Montana on the Wyatt ranch itself, he could be a proper parent.

She knew with her head, that Beck would eventually be fine with Billy, too. If she didn't over analyze Billy's career, she had to admit that he was successful in his chosen field. He was also a man from a close-knit family. He had one brother that would soon be a father. He had two sisters-in-law he could go to should he need input from a grounded female.

Erika was no longer needed, not in the way she'd been needed a month ago. And she'd accomplished what she had set out to do. She was free to go. And she ought to go. She had so much to do back home, and the most practical thing was return to her life with that ever present looming deadline.

But she was loath to leave Beck. She'd miss his warmth and the cuddles. She'd miss his smell and his big toothless smile. She'd miss his blue eyes and the way he splashed in his bath, slapping the water as hard as he could just to make her laugh. Beck had somehow crawled into her heart and it was going to hurt, letting him go.

It would be hard, too, returning to her life in Riverside after this month of baby kisses and company. In California, she lived a quiet life without people, a life where she sat hunched over her desk for hours and hours at a time. Computer, books, online articles, writing. It wasn't meant to be punitive, but it had begun to feel that way. Just spending time with the Wyatts had made her realize how much she missed family and friends… people.

But Beck wasn't hers, and Billy had been April's, and Erika did need to settle back in to her routine. She needed to ask Billy just when they should make the break and how. Because, clearly, she wouldn't get anything done that she needed done here, while trying to survive on the peripheral of Billy Wyatt's life.

※

BILLY DIDN'T THINK he'd ever ridden worse. Not even a full second on the bronc and he was thrown off, landing unceremoniously on his butt. He picked himself up, grabbed his hat, brushed off his dusty backside, and headed for the wooden gate. That was a disappointment. He wouldn't place for money, not in that event. He needed to do better next event. A lot better.

Fellow cowboys patted him on the shoulder as he passed, giving him the same encouragement he gave others. This was a competitive sport, but the guys were mostly class acts. There were a few donkeys out there, but he had a lot of friends in the sport, not counting his best friends, his brothers.

Now he just needed to get his head right, and get his attention back, not easy after the blowup with Erika.

He rarely got angry, and he almost never lost his cool, but she'd pushed his buttons this morning, and he was still riled up.

He wasn't here because he had nothing to do. He was here because this was his job, and how he made money, and the last thing he needed was some prissy prim shrink-wannabe telling him what he needed to do.

He knew what he needed to do, and it was provide for

his son. He wasn't going solo anymore. He was a father. A family man. And he was going to make sure his son could do whatever he wanted in life, including going to college. College was expensive. Graduate school was probably even more. Billy was determined that Beck would get every opportunity in the world, from going to college, to med school or law school. His son would be given tremendous support to make sure he'd always succeed and he didn't need Erika hovering over his shoulder telling him everything he needed to do.

Maybe it was time she moved on.

He appreciated her help but he'd find a way to manage from now on.

Chapter Five

Erika wasn't surprised when Billy showed up on her motel doorstep late in the day. He wasn't smiling, either, and she thought it was the first time she'd ever seen him truly angry.

She'd replayed their argument at the fairgrounds over and over in her head, and thought Billy had been incredibly arrogant and rude, but she hadn't been very diplomatic, either. She was about to apologize when he launched into a verbal firestorm, blaming her for his terrible day. Apparently, he hadn't had that bad of a day in years. It was embarrassing and this was exactly why he needed time to mentally prepare for his events. He couldn't afford to make stupid mistakes, and he couldn't be worrying about Erika and Beck just before he climbed on the back of a bronc or bull.

She listened to him in silence until he abruptly stopped talking. But even after he'd finished, tension filled the room, a hum of hostility that she could feel all the way to her bones. "Is there anything else you'd like to say?" she asked, tone icy.

"Do you understand what I'm saying?"

"I understand that your time before you compete is sacred—"

"You're deliberately provoking me."

"No. I'm not. I don't like fighting, and I don't want to fight with you."

"Good, because I grew up fist fighting with kids at school, as well as my brothers, but I don't argue with women—"

"There. That. Why do you say it like 'Argue with women'? You make it sound like we're an entirely different species."

"I was just raised not to be disrespectful, and I try not to be."

She stepped outside the motel room, not wanting to subject Beck to their quarrel. "You have a very shallow idea of gallantry. I'd far rather a man be straight with me than hold my arm as I cross the street because he thinks I'm weak."

His arms folded over his chest. "Now you're twisting my words."

"I just want us to have an honest conversation."

"Let's do it. Tell me what's upset you."

"I thought you'd said last Sunday that if I came along, and helped care for Beck, it would be a win-win, but so far, it's just a win for you. There is no win for me."

"Because I haven't paid you yet?"

"No, and I don't want to be paid for spending time with Beck. But I do want you to take your share of childcare so I can take care of my job, which is writing my dissertation. I have not had any time this week to do it. Or the week before, or the week before that."

"You can't write when he naps?"

"I maybe could if he had a set nap schedule, but it's constantly changing and it's not easy to sit down and focus on cue. I'd get a lot more done if I knew that he'd be taken care of for three hours, or four hours, and then maybe I wouldn't worry about him, or worry about being interrupted, and I could actually get something accomplished."

"I don't know that I can give you four hours uninterrupted every day—"

"Why not?"

"The point is I can help, but you have to be flexible—"

"I have to be flexible? Billy, all I am is flexible! You're the one that sets the schedule, a schedule we all have to revolve around."

"I don't want to do this. I've no desire to keep fighting. If you're this unhappy, let's not try to make this work."

"Fine. I'm out. Good luck, Billy. You'll need it."

It didn't take her long to pack, not when she just threw everything in a heap into the middle of her suitcase. It took even less time to gather her computer, her books and papers, shoving them into her big leather satchel. Erika stalked to the motel room door, pausing on the threshold to look at Beck, lying on his back on a blanket on the floor, playing with a soft fabric book. Her heart squeezed tight. She wanted to go over and kiss him goodbye but knew she couldn't handle it. She'd fall apart. And she was not going to cry in front of Billy Dickhead Wyatt.

Instead, head high, she walked out the motel door, stepping pointedly around Billy who stood like an ice sculpture outside the room, and headed for the parking lot, where she put her suitcase in the trunk of her car, climbed behind the steering wheel, and drove away without a glance back.

Billy was now on his own.

❦

THE FIGHT WAS stupid. Billy hadn't even seen it coming. One minute they were talking about logistics, and how to make things work, and the next minute, hard, brutal things were being said, and then Erika was grabbing her things and leaving.

And leaving Beck behind.

It was a shock, and her knee-jerk reaction made him livid, but in that moment she marched out to her car and drove away, Billy was glad.

He was *glad* to be rid of her, and rid of her opinions, and her endless pious, Miss Perfect judgment. He didn't need her to make him feel worse. He was already trying to sort through all of his emotions, as it was a lot to take in over a few days. Learning that he was a dad. Learning that April had died in such a tragic accident. Learning that he'd have to overnight become a single parent to a child he'd had no relationship with.

It wasn't that he couldn't do it, either. It was just that it took some adjusting to. Mentally. He needed time to wrap his head around, well, everything.

And if she—this want-to-be therapist—couldn't give him time to adjust, then she wasn't cut out to be a therapist, never mind a friend.

Erika had had a month to come to terms with everything he'd only just learned this past week. She had a month. She'd given him what… days?

It wasn't just unfair, it was unrealistic. And this was why he didn't like therapists. He didn't like the whole get analyzed and explore all your feelings and relive a painful childhood. Everyone had a painful childhood. Everyone got beat up. Everyone was hurt and disappointed. Dammit, people were people and they failed each other all the time.

Best way to deal with disappointment was to grow up and get some perspective. Life could be shitty, but it could also be beautiful and exciting and that was the challenge. Balance the bad with the good, and try to squeeze in more good. Make sure to find all the little happy bits so that you were aware of the blessings. And the joy. As rough and broken as they might be.

It was what his mom had done after his dad died, and it was what Granddad had taught them as well. Feelings could only take you so far. The best thing one could do was get dressed and straighten their damn shoulders and face the day.

And that was what Billy did, every single day.

And that was what he'd do now, with his son.

Billy entered the motel room, and sat down on the carpet next to his son who was now sucking on the spine of his fabric book while waving his legs in the air.

Billy tugged on the soft terry cloth fabric covering Beck's toes, bunching the pale blue fabric. Cute little guy. But of course he was. He was a Wyatt.

⁓

Erika drove away from the motel angry, so angry. She drove, silently cursing Billy, using every inappropriate swear word there was. She understood he had a career, she understood he needed to earn money. That was a given. Everyone had jobs and bills. And she wasn't asking him to sacrifice the entire next year. She just wanted him to focus on Beck for a bit. Why was it all or nothing? Why couldn't he be a competitive cowboy and a hands-on dad?

He could compete next month, or next fall, or heck, next year. Taking off a few weeks, or months, to spend time with his baby wouldn't end his career, but it would be vital for Beck's growth and emotional health.

Whether he liked it or not, Billy was a father, and he needed to bond with Beck. He needed to be present and available, to help Beck feel safe and loved. To create a deep attachment without fear of abandonment. But so far it seemed that Billy was more interested in putting on his chaps and hat than becoming a nurturing parent. So typical of a man, though. They always put themselves first, always saw the world exclusively through their masculine lens.

Maybe one hundred years ago that was fine, but women today were also working full-time and women shouldn't have to shoulder domestic pressures alone. A man could cook and clean and do laundry and childcare just as well as a woman—

Erika glanced down at her speedometer and saw that she was flying down the highway, driving way too fast. She eased her foot off the accelerator, realizing she was shaking. This wasn't okay. Just because she was upset didn't mean she could lose all control. The fact that she lost her temper with Billy made her feel even worse. Erika prided herself on her self-control. She'd grown up determined not to be volatile like her mom, or detached and distant like her dad. And yet she'd just blown up, the way her mom used to, and shouted at Billy, just the way her mom once shouted at her dad.

Ugh.

Awful.

Erika felt awful.

At the next highway exit she pulled off and sat on the shoulder of the frontage road fighting hot tears.

She couldn't believe she'd just driven off and left Beck, too. It was absurd. Immature. Hurtful. It was fine to have emotions—everyone had them—but it wasn't okay to have a tantrum. And it was definitely not okay to walk out on Beck like she did. How childish could she be?

Blinking hard, she reached into her purse for a tissue and wiped her eyes, and beneath her eyes where mascara had made little black smudges, and then with gritted teeth shifted out of PARK, crossed the highway on the overpass, and headed back the direction she just came.

She had to return. She owed Billy an apology, and she owed Beck more than just walking out in a temper.

That was what her parents did. Lost control. Raged. Hurled accusations. Stormed off. Returned and retaliated with days of icy, punishing silence. Then repeated the cycle over and over again. There was a reason she didn't want to be like either of them. It was a terrible way to live and a damaging way to interact with others.

She could do better. She would do better. But first, she needed to apologize. And maybe, just maybe, set healthier boundaries because she didn't like who she was when she lost control.

Thankfully, Billy was at the motel when she returned. Erika was glad. She was also glad she'd turned around when she had because she hadn't been gone long enough for Billy to pack up Beck and leave. No, she was just gone long enough to be mortified by her dramatic, childish tantrum and exit.

If Billy was surprised to see her at the motel door, he didn't reveal it. He was kind enough not to say anything sarcastic, either. "Hello."

As she stood on the doorstep her cheeks felt hot and her insides felt shivery and sick. "That was totally immature of me—"

"It's not a big deal."

"No, it is. I'm sorry. I hate what I just did."

"It's okay."

"No, it's not. It was awful and I'm so embarrassed. I'm sorry."

"I owe you an apology as well. I've not communicated very well with you and I can see how it's made everything so much harder. I promise to work on it, and try to give you more time to work on your dissertation."

Gratitude and relief washed through her. Thank goodness he was handling the fight better than she'd expected. Driving back, she'd worried things would only escalate when she returned. She was glad he wasn't like her dad. No icy silence from Billy. "I understand in theory how to handle conflict, but in reality, I'm not very good at it. I think those of you with siblings probably have more experience with disagreements."

He opened the door wider. "It's okay. Honestly."

She hesitated on the threshold. "I've gotten mad at you twice today."

"With three brothers, I had people mad at me all day long. It's not a biggie."

"Why are you being so nice?"

"Because we're human. People have emotions. Tempers.

People get mad at each other, hurt each other's feelings."

And suddenly eyes that had been so dry filled with tears. Erika bit hard into her bottom lip, trying to stop the tears. "You should be the therapist, not me."

He laughed, the sound warm, husky. "Never. I would hate listening to people's problems all day. I'd tell them to buck up and just get it done."

Erika couldn't help smiling as she wiped her eyes dry. "You wouldn't make as much money."

He laughed again. "That's alright. At least I'd have my sanity. Now come in. This is your room. Relax."

She came in and crouched next to Beck who'd fallen asleep on his blanket on the floor. "I felt terrible leaving him." She lightly stroked the top of his head. "Made me feel sick."

"Then don't leave him."

She looked up at Billy. "I have to one day."

Billy said nothing and she rose, trying to ignore the awful feeling weighting her chest. Everything was getting so complicated. She'd cared for Beck for five weeks now and it seemed inconceivable that soon he wouldn't be in her life.

She could feel Billy's gaze as she went to the edge of the bed and sat down. "If you haven't figured it out yet, I'm not as together as I look. Underneath all this—" she gestured to her head and then the rest of her "—I'm kind of a mess. I probably shouldn't become a therapist, because I have no idea what a healthy marriage or a healthy family looks like. I certainly didn't come from one."

"No one is perfect, and no family is perfect."

"Yours seems pretty perfect in comparison to mine. My family is, well, complicated."

She pursed her lips, considered her words. "My mom's side of the family is from Utah, a little town that no one has ever heard of. Almost everyone in the town belongs to the same church. They're Fundamentalists and part of a tiny Mormon sect with about one hundred and fifty members. The sect isn't recognized by the Church of Latter-day Saints, and wouldn't have been since early twentieth century. It's also very strict, and my mom and April's mom, Aunt Sara, were raised by my grandparents who were involved in the church. My grandfather only did business with other members, and my mom and Aunt Sara were only allowed to socialize with other Fundamentalist girls. They didn't wear modern clothing, either, and they weren't allowed to date, not unless the boy expressed intention to court for marriage, and then they were closely chaperoned. Many, if not all of the young people, had arranged marriages, and my mom and Aunt Sara were expected to have one as well."

"It didn't happen, did it?"

She shook her head. "Aunt Sara got pregnant by a man outside the church. She ended up marrying him, but he was abusive, so she left him and moved to Las Vegas where she raised April with a series of different stepdads and bad boyfriends. My mom met my dad at the community college when she was just nineteen or twenty, and they got married and moved to California. My grandparents cut off both their daughters. I never knew my grandparents and never visited their town, either."

"My family has struggled at different times."

"But you love each other, and talk to each other, and listen. You also forgive each other when someone makes a mistake, don't you?"

"So far."

"Mom didn't have that growing up, and she found it really difficult being a wife and mom." Erika paused, remembering. "I think I'm worried that's my future, too. I think that was the appeal of psychology. Maybe I could learn how to fix myself, while I learned how to help others."

"You don't need fixing."

"I stormed off earlier. It wasn't mature."

"I don't hold it against you."

"I hold it against me. I should know better. I should be able to do better."

He was silent a long moment. "I think you're way too hard on yourself."

Erika shook her head, uncomfortable, wishing they hadn't even discussed any of her family, or her past. It never failed to make her feel bad. There had been so much conflict, and so much unhappiness. She hated remembering because it stirred up all the old feelings and all the old pain. "I don't know that either of them particularly liked me." She lifted her shoulders and let them fall. "I looked too much like my mom, but thought too much like my dad. I was a perfect blend of the two, which didn't sit well with either of them."

"That's ridiculous."

"I just wish I'd know then that I wasn't responsible for their unhappiness. I thought it was my job to fix things, and I couldn't."

BILLY SUDDENLY UNDERSTOOD her so much better. He now understood why she'd studied psychology and counseling. He understood why she'd been so determined to reunite Beck with him. He also understood why she hadn't believed she could manage raising Beck on her own.

She didn't believe she could.

She didn't think she had value.

She saw herself as inherently broken.

And it killed him because she was undoubtedly one of the kindest, strongest, most generous women he'd ever met. She asked for little for herself, and yet when she made a mistake, beat herself up endlessly. "What about you and April?" he asked. "Were you close growing up?"

"We used to see each other at Christmas and other holidays as Aunt Sara would try to join us at Christmas, but as we grew older, and Aunt Sara's boyfriends grew worse, Dad didn't want Sara over. Sara and April were always welcome, but not Sara's boyfriends."

"So Sara stopped coming."

Erika nodded, her eyes, such an unusual mix of green and blue that they looked different every day, narrowed. "By the time we were teenagers, April and I had very little contact. I didn't even know I was her emergency contact until they called me after her accident. I feel bad—"

"About everything," he said, cutting her off. "I know."

"That's not fair," she protested.

"Maybe not, but I have a feeling it's pretty accurate."

She lifted her head and looked at him, brow creasing. Thick golden hair framed her stunning face. He wondered if she had any idea of just how beautiful she was, inside and out. If she wasn't Beck's person, he'd find it awfully hard to keep his distance. But Beck didn't just need him, he needed her, and Erika wasn't the kind of woman you took to bed and then kicked out the next morning, and that was the only kind of woman he got involved with because just as she knew her limitations, he knew his. He wasn't relationship material. He cared about people, but he didn't love, not deeply love, not the way a woman wanted to be loved.

"Why are you being so nice to me?" she asked huskily.

"Everyone should be this nice to you. You're a really good person, Erika Baylor."

Her mouth curved and then trembled. "Am I?"

He nodded, a peculiar pang in his chest. "One in a million."

ERIKA WENT TO bed and dreamed sweet dreams. Billy had made her feel good last night, something remarkable considering their fight earlier. After she lost her cool, she usually hated herself for a long time, loathing her lack of control, loathing her inability to handle difficult situations. But Billy had been kind to her and comforting, as well. He'd managed to help salvage an evening that could have been disastrous. She was grateful. However, his insights into her were a little too accurate, and a little too unsettling, but since he didn't seem to mind that she was flawed, then she was going to let go of everything and just try to move forward.

She certainly moved forward in her dreams. She dreamed that she and Billy were together—not necessarily a couple—but they were hanging out and things were fun and there was no Beck. It was just them and they were driving through mountains and everything was bright and glazed with sunshine. She was laughing at something he said and then somehow they were parked and he was kissing her, really kissing her and she was on his lap and she'd never been kissed like that before, where everything felt so good, and so warm, and so perfect.

She woke up still warm, and happy, feeling relaxed, as well as loved.

And then she realized she was in the dark motel room and that warm glowing buoyant feeling was from a dream. There was no wonderful drive through mountains, no gilded light, no wind in her hair, no kiss that made her feel like she was made of glitter and sunshine.

Her eyes burned and she pressed the pillow over her face, overwhelmed by a disappointment she didn't understand.

TWO HOURS LATER, Erika was changing Beck's diaper when Billy texted.

"I'll have a ticket for you at WILL CALL if you want to come today. I understand if you don't. Either way, let's go out to eat tonight. Craving a good steak."

The wobbly sensation returned to her insides, and she felt a little glimmer of the sun she'd felt in her dream. It wasn't a date tonight but it did sound fun to go out and have a meal somewhere besides her motel room.

She texted back an answer. *"Beck and I will be in the stands cheering for you. Good luck!"*

It was different arriving at the rodeo fairgrounds today. She felt as if she belonged there, and today, all the fans looked friendly and almost familiar. Erika found herself wishing she had a cowboy hat to wear, just so she could be part of the fun. But Beck's dad would be competing, and so was his uncle. Despite Billy's bad day yesterday, he'd still made it into the finals of a couple of his events, and Erika headed for her seat, determined to keep her distance from Billy today so he could concentrate and prepare for his first event.

Seated, she listened to the crowd chatter around her.

Everyone was in a good mood. The weather was cooperating with sun and little wind. Erika had forgotten the baby carrier, so she just sat Beck on her lap, and he was happily eating his fist.

Yesterday she'd missed the opening ceremonies but today she saw it all, and then the first event was announced and Erika's pulse drummed, aware that Tommy would be riding soon. Billy had told her last night that Tommy was having a great weekend, having placed in the finals in every single event he'd entered. She was excited that she'd have two Wyatts to cheer on today, and Tommy did have an excellent time in his first event. The other cowboys, though, didn't look so lucky. Most were bucked off right and left, few making the eight second buzzer. The challenging rides continued through the early afternoon. It didn't seem to matter if it was a horse or bull, but the rodeo clown and announcers made it all entertaining, and Erika was surprised she was enjoying herself so much.

Then finally it was Billy's turn, and he came flying out of the narrow chute on the big chestnut horse, the bronc jumped and bucked, hind legs flying. It was simultaneously spectacular and thrilling as the horse and Billy went up, down, the horse kicking up back legs so high, he went down—all the way to the ground, the horse rolling over on Billy, with Billy still tangled in one stirrup. The crowd gasped and surged to their feet and Erika was on her feet, too.

As if in slow motion, she saw the bronc's hooves connect with Billy, as they both tried to escape each other. Then the horse was free, still bucking and kicking. Billy struggled to get to his feet but crumpled back to the ground, dirt clouding around him. That was when the crowd went silent, and everyone stood in silence as medics ran out.

Gradually, everyone around her began sitting back down, and Erika slowly sat, too, heart in her throat. Seeing Billy on the ground sent panic through her.

Beck needed his dad.

She needed Beck's dad.

Billy had to be okay.

Tommy was out there in the arena now, too, and Tommy and one of the medics assisted Billy to his feet, but Billy couldn't straighten. He stood hunched, his torso bent, left arm hanging limply. He lifted his right hand to the crowd in an attempt to wave, as if reassuring the fans he was fine, but he would have fallen if it weren't for Tommy holding him up.

Billy was half carried, half dragged from the ring, disappearing behind the tall gates that shut behind him, blocking the view.

The crowd was still quiet and the announcers in the high box began their cheerful chatter again, smoothing over the frightening scene, talking about what a cowboy Billy Wyatt was, that all of the Wyatts were true cowboys, and that the announcer had had the privilege of knowing Billy's father,

JC Wyatt, a legend in his time.

Erika tuned out the announcer and tried to think what she should do. Beck made a little peeping sound and she nodded. Beck was right. Find Billy. That was what she needed to do. With trembling hands, she gathered their things, shifted Beck to the other arm, and made her way through the stands, past the snack and food stands, to the pens where livestock waited. She knew now where the cowboys warmed up, and she went there, slipping between cowboys, heading toward an open ambulance that had someone on the gurney in back. She spotted Tommy then, standing near the ambulance talking to someone in a blue chambray shirt with a stethoscope around his neck. Tommy looked grim, nodding once, and then his head turned and his gaze met hers. He said something to the man and then walked toward her.

"He's going to be okay," Tommy said, without preamble. "They're taking him to the hospital in town, and it's serious, but doc doesn't think it's life-threatening. They're leaving now, though, and they'll call me later with updates."

She looked up into his face, trying to read his expression. "You're not going?"

"No."

"What are you going to do?"

"Compete."

She didn't understand. The brothers were close, almost inseparable. "You're still going to ride, even with Billy hurt?"

"He's going to be in surgery. It will be hours. There's nothing I can do until later." Tommy must have seen her confusion, because he added, "This is our agreement. This is what we do. If it's life-threatening, the other goes. If it's just some broken bones, punctured lung—"

"Punctured lung?"

"We carry on. It's the only way competing makes sense. Otherwise, we'd never get any wins, or money, under our belt."

"Should I go to the hospital?"

Tommy glanced from her down to Beck, who was chewing his hand. "And do what?" he asked, tone kind. "You're going to sit around all day, in a germ-filled waiting room. It will be hours before Billy's out of surgery. Then he'd be in recovery, and they'll be monitoring him as he wakes up. Might as well stay here, in the sunshine, soaking up vitamin D, and then when I'm done, I'll drive you over. We'll go together. I promise that that's what Billy would want, too."

It made sense, in a horrible sort of way. "Does this happen often?" she asked, heartsick, because to be honest, it hadn't crossed her mind that they'd get hurt very often. They were both so successful that it seemed as if they had a pretty good handle on how competition worked.

"Often enough we have the drill down. Going to the hospital is never cheap, either. No one likes to get hurt. That's not why we ride and rope. We're trying to earn money, not spend it."

"Are you sure I shouldn't—"

He nodded. "I'm sure. And I promise we will go straight away when I'm done. I'll be finished long before Billy is out of recovery."

Erika returned to the stands but her heart wasn't in it anymore. The afternoon passed slowly, and what had been so exciting earlier, now filled her with dread. It didn't help that all she could think about was Billy, and wondering about his surgery and how he was doing.

It was late when Tommy found her in the stands. "Ready?" he asked.

She nodded, more than ready. Tommy took Beck from her and they walked out of the rodeo grounds together. "Should we take your car since it has the car seat already in it?"

"Sure."

"I'll drive, though," he said. "I know Boise probably better than you."

"I know the motel, and the fairgrounds, and that's it."

He flashed her a smile. "Sounds like you need to get out more."

"Tell that to your brother."

"I will."

She unlocked the car as they approached it, and then handed him the keys. "Have you heard from the hospital?"

He nodded as he opened the door for her, so that she could buckle Beck in. "He's awake, grouchy as a bear."

"Surgery went well?" she asked, stepping back.

He closed the door and then opened her door. "Seems so."

Erika slid into the passenger seat and pulled the seat belt across her. "Are you sure this doesn't happen often?"

Tommy didn't answer until he was behind the steering wheel and typing the hospital's address into his phone. "We've been lucky." He paused. "For the most part."

"It was terrible to watch."

"The majority of injuries occur during rough stock events."

"Rough stock?"

"Bull riding, bareback riding, and saddle bronc riding." Tommy shifted into gear, and followed the GPS directions which indicated that it would take them about fifteen minutes to get across town. Neither of them said much on the way, and it wasn't until Tommy had found a spot in the parking lot that she asked him if he was worried about Billy. "You have to be a little bit concerned?"

Tommy shrugged as he stepped out of the car. "Every injury makes it a little harder to stay in the game, so there's that."

She shouldered Beck and fell into step with Tommy's long strides. "And?"

"Billy's going to be bummed. He was having a good year."

"He's done for the year?"

"I didn't say that. But no one wants to miss a week, much less a month or two, and he's going to miss a fair amount of time. Just how long is yet to be seen."

❧

THE DOCTORS SPOKE to Tommy, not her, which made sense as she wasn't family, but she stood off by the tan vinyl chairs, gently bouncing Beck to keep him asleep as she strained to hear what the surgeon was telling Billy's brother. Tommy looked grave, but not horrified or distraught—not that the Wyatt brothers would ever look distraught—so the update couldn't have been a complete shock to Tommy.

Tommy joined her a few minutes later and filled her in quickly, so quickly that she struggled to process it all. Clavicle fracture, scapula fracture, broken ribs, punctured lungs. Surgery repaired the broken bones, displacement, and lungs. Billy was out of recovery in a room now, but still heavily sedated since he'd done some thrashing about when he first woke up and so he was sleeping now, which the doctor thought was a good thing.

Erika's brow creased as Tommy spoke, her frown deepening as he continued through the litany of injuries. "He'll recover, right?"

"Oh, yeah. He'll be back in the saddle late summer."

Her jaw dropped. "You're kidding."

"Knowing my brother, he'll want to be competing sooner. It just depends on his rehab."

"Where will he go for rehab?"

"Oh, he won't. He'll just do it at home. Billy's been through this before. We all have. Even though a physical therapist is recommended, we'd rather do the exercises on our own."

"So, he's going back to your ranch."

"No, he'll want to go to his place in Utah. Pulling the trailer, it's about eight and a half hours from here."

Erika stared at him, perplexed. "He must be close to Las Vegas?"

"His place is closer to Bryce. I'm assuming that's where he'd want to go, but I guess we'll need to see what he's thinking when he wakes up." Tommy glanced at his watch. "Why don't I drive you to your hotel so you and Beck can have dinner and relax? I'll worry about Billy."

She hesitated. "I feel bad that I'm not doing anything."

"But what can you do?"

She had no answer for that.

Chapter Six

Billy had been bucked, kicked, rolled on, and stomped on before.

He'd been gored.

He'd been thrown.

He'd been dragged around in the arena, foot caught in ropes.

He'd been afraid before. It was only natural when an animal weighing more than a thousand pounds was doing the stomping, rolling, dragging, and kicking, but this time, this injury was different. This time, as the horse rolled on him, pinning him beneath, he thought of only one thing—his son. Not true, he thought of Beck in Erika's arms, her lovely golden head tipped as she gave the top of his bald head a kiss. And in that moment of stunning pain, Billy knew he had to be okay. His son needed him to be okay. It wouldn't be fair to Erika to disappear on them now.

It was while being transported in the ambulance, and then rushed into surgery, brain cloudy with drugs and pain, he realized something about himself. He was full of bull. He acted like he didn't have a care in the world, when he had many. He loved his mom profoundly, and his grandfather meant everything to him. His brothers were his best friends and he knew that if anything happened to him, the whole family would suffer. They would hurt, and he would never want them to grieve, not for him, or over him. He liked making his mom laugh. He enjoyed being one of her 'bad boys,' not because he was truly bad, but because it made her lips quirk, and her head shake, and yet even then, her eyes would light up with a secret, silent amusement.

But his family were adults, and his brothers were men. They could all fend for themselves. But Beck was just an infant, and he deserved better. He deserved more. Beck had already lost his mother. He shouldn't lose his father.

It was his last thought before he went under the anesthesia, and the first thought when he began to come round in recovery. He was a dad now. He had to do better. Be better. Even groggy, his limbs so heavy he couldn't move, Billy vowed to step up.

But when Erika visited with Beck later that evening, he didn't know how to say any of this, not when his body throbbed, and his head ached, and he felt almost as helpless as Beck.

"Thanks for coming," he said, his voice raspy.

"Of course," she answered, taking a step closer to the bed, the baby on her hip. "How do you feel?"

"How do I look?"

"Pretty rough."

"Makes sense, because that's how I feel."

"That was so scary."

"I'd like to see the film. It happened so fast."

"Have you ever been hurt this badly before?"

"Oh sure, but not often. I've been lucky."

She nodded, but she didn't look reassured.

"I'm sorry you had to see that," he added. "It's one reason my mom wouldn't watch us compete. She said it made her too nervous, what with all the things that could go wrong."

"I totally relate." Erika glanced around, and then looked back at him. "I have to use the restroom—"

"Again?" he teased.

It took her a moment to get the joke and then she shook her head, smiling. "You're incorrigible."

"That's an awfully big word for a man with a concussion." And then he nodded to the small bathroom in the corner of his room. "You could use mine."

"They say not to."

"It's my restroom. The hospital will be billing me for it."

"In that case, can I just leave Beck here with you? I left his car seat in the car, but I can slide him into your good arm." And without waiting for a reply, she tucked the baby into the crook of his uninjured arm, adjusting his hand, with the IV, before disappearing into the bathroom.

When she emerged a few minutes later, he stopped her from taking Beck back. "It's okay," he said. "Leave him with me. It's good to have him here."

She stood uncertainly at his side. "Can I get you anything?"

"Double cheeseburger and fries?"

"*Now?*"

"Probably not now, but I'd love it if you brought me some tomorrow. And a vanilla shake. Large."

Erika slowly smiled until even her eyes crinkled. "I can do that."

"Good." Billy paused. "And thank you."

"For what?"

"For everything." He nodded down at the baby. "But most of all, finding me."

Her smile wasn't completely steady. "You mean that?"

"I do. Beck needs me. I realized earlier that if something happened to me there are others in the family who'd take care of Beck, just as my grandfather stepped in when my dad died. But I don't want others raising my son. I want to raise him. I want to teach him all the things I wish my dad had taught me."

Her expression changed, shadows flickering in her eyes before she managed a smile. "If you mean that, Beck will be the luckiest boy alive."

BACK AT THE hotel that evening Erika gave Beck his dinner and a bath and got him down to bed, but she remained restless and anxious and overly emotional.

She'd been so afraid when Billy had gotten hurt. She'd felt panic, but something else, something like pain. She'd hurt. She'd been afraid for him, but she'd also been afraid for herself, and that didn't make sense. Why should she hurt? She barely knew him. And yet, in that moment where she wasn't afraid he'd live, all she wanted was him in one piece, all she wanted was him to be okay.

She'd maybe even prayed in those terrible moments, and she wasn't one to pray, having been raised by a mom who viewed religion as a special kind of hell, a crutch for people who were too weak to handle life without someone telling them how to think, and who to be.

But she had prayed, because her heart burned, her chest squeezing tight, and she didn't think she'd ever breathe properly if he didn't get up, if he couldn't walk away.

In the end, he was okay, but it had broken something loose inside of her, creating chaos and confusion that hadn't been there before.

She liked Billy Wyatt a lot.

She liked him more than she should.

Her feelings for him were more than just a passing interest and that was a problem. Being near him was becoming a problem. Her dream hadn't come out of nowhere. A part of her had known she was falling for him. A part of her had been warning her and she hadn't been paying attention.

Or maybe she had, and she just didn't want to admit it.

Troubled, she pulled out her computer and set it up on the bed, determined to get some work done. She needed to accomplish something, feel in control of something, but as fifteen minutes turned to thirty, and she was still staring at her screen, her hands in her lap instead of the keyboard, she knew she wasn't going to get anything significant done. Not tonight. Not after today.

The accident had happened so quickly. The chute had opened. The horse had leaped out and then within seconds the horse was rolling over Billy and giving him a kick for good measure.

She hadn't seen the accident coming. Maybe that was why they were called accidents, you didn't expect them, and they came out of nowhere, crashing into reality, destroying all sense of safety, and control.

First April's accident and now this.

Billy could have been killed. He was lucky to just have broken bones and a concussion. Erika closed her computer and placed it on the nightstand. She went to the bathroom to brush her teeth and as she looked at herself in the mirror, she saw the fear and confusion in her eyes.

Billy did this to himself every single weekend. He willingly put himself in danger all year long. It was madness. The man wasn't living in any reality she recognized. And yet the man mattered to her. She wanted to help him. She wanted to protect him. But how?

Erika didn't sleep well. She woke up still anxious and

took Beck on a long morning walk, more for her sake than his. Later, she changed Beck and headed to the hospital, stopping to buy Billy the burgers, fries, and shake he'd requested last night.

She carefully arranged the meal on his rolling hospital tray, before positioning it just so in front of him.

She ignored the way his upper lip quirked at her presentation.

"Want some?" he asked, reaching for a fry.

She shook her head. "Not hungry, thank you."

He ate one of the burgers before speaking again. "You're upset."

"I think I'm still traumatized from yesterday. That was horrible—"

"It's not a big deal."

"No, wrong." She rocked Beck's car seat with her foot. "That was a big deal. You got hurt. You could have died."

"But I didn't. I'm just a little bruised—"

"Not just bruised," she gritted. "Broken bones everywhere."

"They'll mend. I'll be good as new in just a couple weeks."

She stared at him, stunned by his casual dismissal of what had happened in the ring yesterday. "What you do for a living... it's insane. You have to be insane to think it's okay."

"I don't get hurt often."

"That doesn't justify the danger."

"There's danger everywhere. The world is filled with risk—"

"But why invite risk in? Why say, *hey risk, come sit at my table*?" Her gaze searched his. He didn't seem troubled. Or worried. "Billy, Beck doesn't need you in a wheelchair, or worse."

"I have no intention of being in a wheelchair. Or worse. So please don't put that out there. I don't need the negativity."

The negativity.

As if his life depended on sage and crystals.

She ground her jaw together, molars gritted tight. He either didn't understand his value or didn't care. But the world wouldn't be the same without him. Not for Beck.

And not for her.

THE NURSE ENTERED the room to take his vitals and change his urine bag and Erika took advantage of the interruption to make her escape.

"You have a very pretty girlfriend," the nurse said, smiling, as she checked Billy's pulse.

Billy was about to reply that Erika wasn't his girlfriend and then closed his mouth. Because Erika was gorgeous, and he'd been looking forward to her coming this morning and he was sorry she'd left. "Yes, she is."

"That baby's adorable, too. You're a lucky man."

Warmth filled Billy's chest and he nodded. "Thank you," he said gruffly. "I feel lucky." And not just because he'd survived yesterday, but because he had people who cared. His family. Friends. Erika.

He knew Erika cared. He knew she wasn't giving him grief just because she could. She was genuinely concerned, and her concern mattered. The last thing he wanted to do was worry her, but at the same time, he was a professional cowboy, and there were hazards to his occupation, and as much as he didn't want to stress her, he couldn't—wouldn't—change who he was.

The doctor arrived late in the day, and Billy asked all the questions he wanted to know, questions regarding recovery because riding, roping, and competing were central to him. His identity was that of a cowboy. He couldn't remember a time when he wasn't competing. He'd learned back in high school if he competed well, he walked away with trophies, saddles, and belt buckles. As an established name in the PRCA, he earned big money, and now that he was a dad, he needed to provide for his boy. His earnings would give Beck a home.

❦

EVERY DAY ERIKA took Beck to see Billy at the hospital. Billy had his own room which made it easier for visits. Some days she'd have to wait in the hall while nurses did whatever they did in Billy's room, and other times he was alone when she arrived, and he'd reach for Beck, which made her happy.

While Billy held Beck, she'd settle into a chair and chat about whatever Billy wanted to discuss. Sometimes they'd just watch the news on TV, and other times he'd ask her to read something to him on her phone. "Do you need reading glasses?" she asked him the second time he'd requested she look something up for him.

He adjusted Beck in the crook of his arm, so that Beck could sit up properly. "No. I just... don't read well."

She frowned. "But you can read."

"I can. I don't find it easy, though." He paused a beat. "I'm dyslexic. It's not a big thing, just something I deal with."

"I had no idea."

"It's not something I brag about."

"Not something to be ashamed of, either."

"Maybe if I'd been diagnosed younger, there would have been less shame. But I was eleven when I was diagnosed, the end of fifth grade, and by then, I hated school. I'd been labeled lazy and troubled for so many years that school felt like prison. I just didn't want to be there."

She'd studied dyslexia and learning disabilities extensively as part of her program. "How did they finally figure it out?"

"Sam did."

"Your brother Sam?"

"Sam was really good in school, especially with reading and writing. One night after Mom had gotten really mad at me for bad grades, Sam offered to tutor me. It took him about a week to understand what was going on, and he was the first person to figure out that my trouble was seeing the letters. I had a difficult time decoding them. My brain didn't 'see' the whole picture, and then I had trouble remembering what I did read."

"Visual dyslexia."

He nodded. "Once Sam figured it out, the school's special education program was able to confirm it."

"Don't tell me you were put in special ed."

"They didn't think I was very smart."

"That's ridiculous!"

He smiled at her vehement tone. "I'm just glad Sam was able to help me. Sam's smart that way. He's always been focused. Strategic. He'd make a great general."

"And you'd be his foot soldier?"

"I'd follow Sam anywhere." He hesitated, then smiled ruefully. "And I have."

"Do you like his wife?"

"Ivy? She's amazing. She and Sam belong together."

"You like Joe's wife, too."

"Sophie is perfect for Joe."

"Does Tommy have anyone special?"

Billy shook his head. "No. He and I are confirmed bachelors."

Erika was silent a moment processing everything, before asking, "Have you told your family about Beck? That he is your son?"

"I sent a text to everyone. No one was surprised."

"Not even your mom?"

He laughed. "Least of all her. She said she knew it all along."

Erika smiled. "I like her."

"She's a good woman. She put up with all of us." Billy shifted and his hospital gown dipped low on his chest, and peeled up on his arm, revealing more bronzed skin, and hard honed muscles, than she'd ever seen on any man. His jaw was bristled, and his hair shaggy and she looked away every time the covers came up, exposing his knee or thigh, aware that there was nothing on under his cotton gown than bandages and… skin.

"Do you want me to take Beck back?" she asked, her pulse racing a little too fast, her voice sounding a little too breathy.

"No, I'm good. Do I look uncomfortable?"

She glanced back at him, the exposed collarbone on one side, and thick white bandages on the other. Even with cast and sling he looked amazing. Physical, virile, male. Incredibly male. Incredibly sexy. "I just don't want to tire you out."

"You haven't even been here a half hour."

"I've been warned not to stay too long."

"By whom? I'll have a word with that person."

"That's not necessary. Everyone is just trying to take good care of you."

"I feel great. I'm just bored, and ready to go home."

"Doesn't Tommy come see you?"

"He does, but he can't really stay long. He's taking care of both of our horses, and they all need exercise, food, and attention."

"What's his plan? Where will he go from here?"

"He'll get me home and then take off, heading to the next rodeo."

Erika sat up a little taller. "About that… home to Montana, or home to…?"

"Utah."

She was just about to ask another question when the door opened, and Sam entered the room. Billy grinned at his older brother. Sam moved in for a careful hug, not wanting to smash Beck or jostle Billy. Erika bit her lip, holding in her smile. There was so much love between brothers. It touched her. Made her feel hope. Beck was lucky to grow up in this family where men weren't afraid to show emotion, or affection.

"What are you doing here?" Billy asked, as Sam straightened.

"Came to help haul your sorry self home," Sam answered, his gaze sweeping Billy, taking in his condition. "You okay to travel?"

"Yes. I was just telling Erika I'm ready to go."

Sam shot Erika a smile. "Has he been a pain?"

"No."

"That's a surprise," he answered before looking back at his brother. "Relax, rest, and know we're going to do our best to break you out tomorrow."

※

THE WYATT BROTHERS had sorted out logistics before Erika could even ask how they intended to get from Boise to Billy's property with multiple vehicles, including two four-wheel drive trucks, her car, two trailers, four horses, an injured cowboy, and a five-month-old baby. But it had been handled, with Sam planning on leaving his truck in Boise to drive Billy's truck and trailer, while Tommy would drive his. Tommy had offered to take Erika and Beck in his truck with him, saying they could get her car later, but she wanted her own car, needed the independence. Besides, she'd driven far longer than eight hours with Beck before and she could certainly handle a long day's drive to Billy's property.

Wednesday morning, four days after Billy's injury, and immediately after Billy was discharged, they were off, with Billy in the passenger seat of the truck Sam was driving, pillows tucked here and there around the bruised and broken places. They set off at ten, a caravan with truck and trailers in front, and Erika in the back, with the expectation that they'd arrive at Billy's house right around dinnertime. She had both Tommy and Sam's phone numbers in case she needed to stop somewhere, but as it turned out, the big trucks pulling big rigs burned through gas a lot faster, and so there were plenty of stops to stretch her legs and feed Beck on the drive south.

It was late afternoon as they left the freeway, taking smaller state roads east. The mountains in the distance were weathered, revealing layers of pink and red. The two-lane highway went down the middle of the valley, with a river on one side and pastures on both. They passed no big towns, driving through towns with just a gas station and, if they were lucky, a café or corner convenience store.

The sun was setting when they pulled through a gate and then down a long road, finally reaching the two-story cabin with a steep green metal roof and large windows. She'd pictured something small and rustic but the cabin was new, the big logs stained dark gold. Once through the front door, the interior was surprisingly airy, with a high-beamed ceiling and tall windows that overlooked the valley. In the distance rose more of those same pink and red mountains.

Sam and Tommy helped get Billy settled into his room. There were two other bedrooms, and Billy had suggested she take the one nearest the living room so she could be closer to the kitchen for making Beck's bottles. Sam said he'd take the couch in the living room, and Tommy could have the third bedroom. Tommy insisted on the couch, saying Sam should have the bedroom since he'd been raised to be respectful of his seniors.

Their back and forth only ended when Erika asked if there was a store nearby because Billy had nothing in his refrigerator for dinner. "Thinking I should get some groceries," she said.

"Good idea," Tommy said. "Billy can eat."

"You can eat," Sam retorted, before looking at Erika. "I can drive you, if you want. I know where the store is."

She glanced into Billy's bedroom where he was already asleep on his bed. Beck was dozing in his car seat. "I'd love that if Tommy is okay managing things here."

"Shouldn't be a problem," Tommy answered, "not if they both stay asleep."

She smiled, amused. "Let's hope they do then. We'll be quick and should return soon."

It seemed as if Sam drove forever, even though it was probably just ten minutes, before pulling over near a nondescript looking café with an even less interesting looking convenient store next door. She glanced out at the businesses and then at Sam. "Doesn't look very encouraging," she said.

"They'll have the basics. Milk, bread, eggs. If we're lucky we'll find some ground beef."

Inside the store, she loaded her basket with the basic essentials, along with a couple bananas, some apples, ground beef, and the only package of chicken breasts in stock. She'd never made Billy a meal before, and wasn't looking forward to trying to make dinner for all the guys tonight. She wasn't a great cook and usually lived off cereal, toasted bagels, and canned soup.

Sam added two bags of egg noodles to the basket, a can of cream of mushroom soup, and a small container of sour cream and then took the basket from her. "Does poor man's stroganoff sound okay?"

"I don't know what it is."

"Tonight's your lucky night," he said, heading for the cash register. "What about Beck? Does he need anything?"

"Not yet. But this weekend I'll probably need to buy formula and diapers."

"If you drive south toward Zion, there's a town with some bigger stores. Or, if you go to the city of Bryce, just east of the park entrance, you'll find everything you need there."

"So, there are some real towns around here."

"Yes. You just have to be willing to drive and know where to find them."

Back at the cabin, Sam unpacked the groceries and began dinner while she checked on the guys. They were all asleep—even Tommy who'd stretched out on the couch, with Beck's car seat parked next to him.

She smiled crookedly, warmth filling her chest. Good thing she wasn't a sucker for a pretty face because the Wyatt brothers all looked far too appealing when paired with a baby.

AFTER DINNER, EVERYONE called it a night, with Beck and Erika disappearing into their room, while the brothers sorted out where they'd crash for the night. Sam and Tommy left after breakfast the next day, trying to make Oklahoma for the weekend's rodeo, with the plan to pick up Sam's truck the following Monday.

After they'd gone, the cabin felt different. Everything became quieter, far less lively.

A little less happy.

Billy spent most of the day in bed in his room, and she'd check in on him, but he was definitely withdrawn.

"Can I get you anything?" she asked midafternoon, popping her head once more around his partially open door. His blinds were down and the room dark with shadows now that the sun had shifted in the sky. She couldn't help feeling worried. He'd had breakfast with his brothers but nothing to eat or drink since then. "Water? Tea? A snack?"

"I'm fine," he answered flatly, before adding on a thank you.

"Anything special you want for dinner?"

"I don't have much of an appetite."

"I thought you liked to eat," she said, approaching the bed.

"I do, but not hungry today."

She reached out and touched his forehead. His skin was smooth. He wasn't feverish. He wasn't cold, either. "Do you think it's the pain meds?"

"Maybe."

"Or your brothers leaving."

For a moment, he said nothing then he let out a raspy laugh. "Am I that pathetic?"

There was no chair in the room and so she sat down on the edge of the bed. Her eyes were adjusting to the dim light, and she could see the light blue of his sling holding his left arm still. "You love them. That's not a bad thing."

"It's hard being left behind. I wanted to be there this weekend."

She bit her tongue to prevent her from answering. She couldn't understand how Billy could even think of competing when he was so badly injured.

"At least Sam will be with Tommy. They'll compete together for the team events, so that's good," Billy added, struggling to sit up.

She rose and adjusted a pillow behind his back. "Do you need another pillow?"

"This bed isn't very comfortable."

"Maybe because you've been in it all day. I bet you could use a change of scenery. You have a very nice leather recliner in the living room."

"Is this your way of telling me you're feeling lonely?"

She choked back a laugh. "In case you haven't noticed, Beck keeps me quite busy."

"And I haven't done much to help out today," he said, swinging his legs out from beneath the covers. His flannel shirt was half on, buttoned over the injured shoulder and arm. An ACE bandage wrapped tightly around his rips, giving her glimpses of bare skin.

"You get a pass today," she said, smiling. "Now tomorrow, who knows?"

"And Beck? How is he?"

"He's been napping but I think he's waking up."

"Does he need a bottle?"

"He will." She watched him rise. He swayed a little on his feet. She nearly reached out to help him but stopped herself in time. "You okay?"

"Fine. Just give me a second."

"You don't need an arm on the way to the living room?"

"I have two of my own, and my legs work just fine."

"Okay. I'm going to get Beck up from his nap, change him and then bring him to you for a bottle."

When Erika emerged from her room, Billy was in his leather chair, a pillow wedged beneath his left elbow, the TV on to an early news broadcast.

She positioned Beck on Billy's lap so that he could give the baby a bottle. "You're good?" she asked him, cocking her head, frowning down at him.

"Do I not look good?" he drawled, giving her a look that made her blush.

He was so confident, but also so sexy. It wasn't fair. He was completely out of her league. She had no idea how to manage him. "Fishing for compliments?" she flashed tartly.

"Just wanted to be sure I hadn't lost my charm."

She rolled her eyes. "If you're good, I'd love to go take a shower."

"Take your time. Beck and I are just going to be watching the news."

⁓

AFTER HER SHOWER, Erika heated up the leftover stroganoff for dinner, and then took Beck and put him on a blanket on the floor so Billy could eat.

She'd been worried there might not be enough, but Billy ate his fill, but didn't ask for seconds, which was good, since there wasn't any. She carried the dishes to the kitchen sink to soak and then refilled Billy's tall water cup and brought him the prescription bottle from the kitchen counter. "You're supposed to take this one with food in the evening," she said.

"Thanks."

She pulled the blue gel teething ring out of the diaper bag and handed it to Beck before sitting down on the couch. "Are you hurting?"

"A bit, but I'm holding off the pain meds until I go to bed. I don't like to take them too often. Don't want to get dependent on them. I'll probably stop taking them in another day or so since they make me a little groggy."

"Is groggy bad? You're not supposed to be doing anything but healing right now."

"I've got my horses to care for. Beck that needs attention.

And you," he said, looking straight at her, "have work to do. Work you haven't been able to do. Two weeks in a row now."

She was touched, and appreciated he was thinking of her. "Tomorrow, I'm hoping to get some work done."

"Good."

She was trying to feel optimistic, too, but she was also aware that Billy was limited in what he could do without help. She wasn't even sure what he could do. He hadn't asked her for any assistance today, but she knew his brothers had been like a morning nurse, changing his bandages, aiding him with his sling, before helping him with his shirt, ensuring he was partially dressed before they left. "What will you need me to do for before bed? Any bandages need to be changed?"

"Can you not say it like they're diapers?"

She snorted, and then giggled at her own inelegant snort.

Billy lifted an eyebrow which only made her laugh all over again. Erika didn't know why she was laughing, only that it felt good, and for the first time in a long time, she felt happy. And it was an amazing way to feel.

CHAPTER SEVEN

THE NEXT MORNING, Erika had only just finished making coffee and dressing when Billy appeared in the kitchen in nothing but baggy black sweatpants that hung off his lean hips, revealing a torso of chiseled abs and sinewy muscle. He had bruises across his chest, as well as scars, fresh scars from the recent surgery, and then older ones.

She tried to drag her gaze up to his face, but his body was fascinating. It was an athlete's body, a mature man's body, the embodiment of strength with so much muscle. She found herself wanting to study each hollow and shape, shadow and scar, tracing the lines and planes.

It took every ounce of her discipline to raise her gaze and look him in the eye. "Morning," she said.

"Morning. Hoping you can give me a hand," he said, holding a big Ziploc bag filled with gauze and tape, while stretchy bandages and the blue sling dangled from his fingers.

"Of course. How do you want to do this? What first?"

He set everything on the kitchen island and pulled out a stool and sat down. "Gauze and tape on the surgery wound, and then we'll wrap my chest with the first bandage, and finally the sling."

"Aren't you supposed to have another stretchy bandage on top of the sling, to hold it all in place?"

"I'm not going to worry about it. Keeping the surgical wound clean is key, and then the rib compression thing helps a lot, and so does the sling."

He walked her through covering up the dark red and purple wound on his shoulder. She could still see all the stitches and was glad when it was covered by the gauze, and securely taped.

"Now the ribs," he said, rising. "Just wrap the compression belt around my chest and smooth the Velcro closed."

She'd seen Tommy do this yesterday and had a general idea of what she'd need to do, but somehow it was different when she was the one standing in front of him. "You can't lift your arms, can you?"

"Not the left one. You'll need to get close, slide it up under my elbow and pull tight."

She was facing him, almost hip to hip, torso to torso and she could feel his warmth, heat radiating off of him. Admittedly, the cabin was warm. Billy liked setting the thermostat at a comfortable temperature, to keep him from aching from cold when he wasn't moving. But confronting Billy's bare chest, and broad shoulders, and narrow waist made her throat dry, and her heart do weird little skips.

"I probably have coffee breath," she warned.

"I like coffee."

Her face grew hot, and butterflies filled her middle as she took the wide stretchy compression belt from the counter. She slid it around his waist and then lifted it up his torso until she could pull it tightly closed. Her nose was almost pressed to his chest and he smelled amazing, skin and a hint of soap, or body wash, but whatever it was, it was delicious. He smelled delicious. It'd be so easy to put a little tiny kiss there, right between his pecs, but she stopped herself from going down that path.

"Sling next?" she asked huskily.

He sat back down on the stool, and she had to step between his legs to slip the strap around his neck. "I don't want to hurt you," she said.

"You won't," he answered, "at least not more than I already hurt."

She looked up into his blue eyes. They were exactly the same shade as Beck's. "You're in pain now?"

"I tried to do too much in the shower—" He broke off as she arched an eyebrow. "Do you have a dirty mind?"

"*No.*" Erika blushed and vigorously shook her head, and yet they were so close, and he was so warm and there was something powerful in the close proximity, something intoxicating. "I—" She broke off, and bit into her lower lip. "Nothing. Let's just get you dressed."

She helped ease his left elbow into the blue sling, drawing the strap through and pulling it taut, stopping when

Billy told her that it was good. She had to lean in to press the Velcro pieces together, ensuring a snug fit, and with her nose practically in the side of his neck, her heart raced, her pulse pounding, even as desire coiled in the pit of her stomach, making her feel breathless. Dizzy.

She peeked up at his mouth. He had firm lips, just full enough to make her think he'd know how to kiss. But of course he'd know how to kiss. He knew how to do everything. It was why women flocked to see him in every town.

Usually that would be enough to pull her back, bring her to her senses, but this morning she didn't want to move away. This morning she wanted to move in.

She wanted to touch him, feel him, feel his mouth on hers.

She couldn't ever remember wanting to be kissed this badly.

But just wanting something didn't make it right, or realistic, and she needed to remain in reality. Firmly rooted in reality. She couldn't afford to be one of those women who lost their head over a hot guy with great pheromones.

"You could probably use some clothes at this point," she said, heart still racing, voice unsteady. "Is there a shirt or sweatshirt I could grab for you?"

"There's a light gray sweatshirt hanging on a hook by the front door. I'll take that one."

It was a short walk to the door, and there was only one sweatshirt on the coat hooks. She lifted it off, glad to see it had a zipper, and carried it back to him. Billy took the sweatshirt from her, slid his right arm into the right sleeve, and then sat still while she helped draw the left side over his immobile shoulder and arm.

But just lifting his right arm had exposed more of his magnificent torso, the thick compression band doing more to define the thick muscles in his back than hide them. His hard, carved abs appeared below the edge of the compression garment, disappearing into the waistband of his sweats. He had an eight-pack at the very least. She wouldn't let herself count them all, only that his body was ridiculously hot and she understood why women wanted it. *Him.*

She did, too.

Just a kiss, and maybe—

"If you could just tug the fabric over the left shoulder a bit more, we should be able to zip the sweatshirt closed," he said.

Erika was having a hard time processing what he was saying. She looked into his eyes, needing him to repeat the instructions. His intensely blue eyes seemed to be looking all the way through her, straight into her heart and soul. He wasn't smiling either, and a tiny shiver raced through her, making her skin sensitive all over.

"Just adjust the left shoulder," he said, his voice pitched deep. "Zip it up, as far as you can, and I'll be good for the day."

Her hand shook ever so slightly as she connected the

sweatshirt at the hem, hooking the zipper threads. She drew the zipper up, closing the soft cotton fabric over his chest. "How's that?" she asked, stopping zipping halfway between the hard planes of his chest. "Or do you want it higher? Not sure how much movement you need."

"You could take it up another inch," he said.

Again, her gaze met his and her breath caught in her throat, emotions flitting through her—desire, curiosity, need. She reached up to zip another inch, her face so close to his chest that she felt surrounded by his powerful body, cocooned by his warmth and scent. Zipper sorted, she adjusted the sling strap a fraction of an inch, her fingertips brushing his chest. He was all muscle and firm, and her insides felt wobbly with want. "What soap did you use?"

"Whatever was in there. I think it's just a bar of soap. You don't like it?"

"No. It's nice. You smell good."

"Thank you."

He smelled better than good but she wasn't going to tell him that, just as she wasn't going to tell him how much she wanted to kiss him, just to brush her lips over his, and see what it felt like, see if she liked it.

Maybe he wasn't a good kisser.

Maybe he didn't kiss the way she wanted.

She almost hoped so, because right now she found him virtually irresistible.

"All good?" he asked.

She forced herself to give him a brisk pat on his chest before stepping backward. Erika ignored the fact that her legs were embarrassingly weak. Just like her insides felt weak and shivery, and her lower back felt tingly. "There you are. Good to go."

"Thank you."

She managed a smile, hoping it looked serene. "How about some coffee?"

"I'd love some. Does Beck need a bottle?"

"He had one earlier. He should be good for a bit."

"What about breakfast then?"

Erika frowned. "For Beck?"

"For us. Aren't you hungry?"

"I'll probably have something later. I don't eat right away—" She broke off, realizing what he was saying. Billy was hungry. "You eat breakfast."

"I like breakfast," he agreed, prolonging the conversation.

※

BILLY WASN'T READY to let her escape and move to a different room. He liked having her close. She made the morning feel special, as if it was a big weekend, or a family holiday.

Erika had always been pretty in a don't-touch-me sort of way, making him feel as though she was too educated, too polished, too sophisticated for a cowboy like him. But when she'd helped him with the bandages and then his sweatshirt, he'd seen something different in her eyes. She'd been softer, warmer. Approachable.

He'd been tempted to reach for her and pull her closer to him, drawing her more snugly between his thighs so that he could feel her against him. He wanted to trace the line of her jaw and tilt her head up to kiss the hollow beneath her ear, and then lower, along the side of her neck. He wanted to feel her breasts against his chest, and let her bottom fill his hands. She was very much a woman, and her curves and softness called to him. She was so pretty, so smart, so appealing, and yet he respected her too much to make a move. He couldn't risk hurting her, or alienating her, not when Beck needed her so much. Far better to deny the attraction than let it get out of hand.

"Normally, I'd make my own breakfast," he said, leaning back against the island, "but it's tough to crack the eggs and do it all one-handed, especially when my ribs are still so sore. Would you be willing to make eggs for me today?"

"Eggs," she repeated.

"We have some, don't we?"

"Half a dozen, I think."

"Perfect."

She hesitated, her brows pulling together. "I…" Her frown deepened. "Um, I don't know how."

"You don't know how to make eggs?"

Her chin lifted a fraction, and she gave him an unsmiling look. "Have I shocked you that much?"

"No."

"Are you testing my domestic skills? Measuring how much I mastered before becoming a woman?"

Billy knew he shouldn't, but he laughed. She was so outraged. "No need to take it so personally. I was just surprised. I thought eggs were pretty basic and something everyone knew how to make."

Her arms folded over her chest. "I don't eat a lot of eggs. I am more of a yogurt for breakfast kind of girl, thank you."

He fought the urge to smile, aware it wouldn't help anything. "You're welcome."

"Are you in need of eggs to start your day?"

"I enjoy a hot breakfast and prefer eggs. Eggs are a good protein, and apparently there's an enzyme in eggs that helps you stay full longer, which is helpful when you're always hungry."

"You're always hungry?"

"I have a fast metabolism," he confessed, amused, and enjoying himself far too much.

He shouldn't like riling her up, but when she was feisty like this, she reminded him of one of his favorite hens, Mrs. Broody, who'd get so mad when any of them entered the chicken coop each morning. Mrs. Broody was the one who'd let out a squawk and then do her best to chase them away. Billy also suspected Erika wouldn't appreciate being compared to a chicken.

"I had no idea," she drawled.

He smiled innocently. "There was no reason to discuss it."

"You'll have to fill me in on all your requirements. Until now, I've been pretty occupied with Beck. Perhaps I should get a notebook and write down your schedule and your nutritional needs."

Billy laughed, the sound filling the kitchen. Erika glared at him. He couldn't remember when he'd last enjoyed himself so much. "I'd hate to overwhelm you," he said. "Why don't we just focus on breakfast, and I'll stay here and give you a little tutorial—"

"Not necessary."

"No trouble at all," he replied, deliberately misunderstanding her meaning. "I'll walk you through scrambled eggs today, and then we could try fried eggs tomorrow."

Her lips compressed and her blue-green eyes blazed at him. He could practically feel her temper rise degree by degree. "How about you walk me through scrambled eggs today," she said through gritted teeth, "and then that's what you get from here on out."

He smiled at her. Most charmingly. "Will I be pushing my luck to ask for some bacon and sausage?"

"I could probably do one or the other. You don't need both."

"You're worried about my cholesterol."

"I'm worried about the work required to feed you."

"Perfectly valid. But could I request toast? If it's not too much trouble? Two slices whole wheat, white, sourdough. Whatever we have with plenty of butter. I like it light brown—"

"Listen Billy, I am not a diner. This is not Erika's Kitchen. You're going to get toast, I can't guarantee it will be the right color, I can't guarantee it will have the right amount of butter. I can't even promise you that it will be warm when I serve it, but you *will* have toast, two eggs—"

"Three?" he interrupted hopefully.

"You eat three eggs every morning?"

He nodded. "And bacon and sausage. Or a nice ham steak."

"So you personally go through a dozen eggs every four days?"

"Sometimes in three days, depending on what else I'm eating."

"How many slices of toast each morning?"

"Two, please." He gave her his sweetest smile.

Her eyes narrowed. She didn't smile back. "So let's get this straight. Three eggs, two bacon, and two slices of toast."

"Or three sausage links and, or, a nice thick ham steak."

"No pork chops?" she snapped sarcastically.

He heard the sarcasm and liked it. Her fire made him hungry and hard. He wanted her even more. She was smart, beautiful, sassy, sexy. So sexy. Which just made him want to tease her more. "I do like grilled pork chops with eggs, very much. We don't have any pork chops, do we?"

"No. No, we don't. Now, how about I scramble the eggs and then you show me how you like them cooked. And no more changing up the order. No more special requests. You get what you get, and don't throw a fit."

"You sound just like my kindergarten teacher, Mrs. Gosnell."

"I imagine you were quite demanding as a five-year-old."

"Tommy was more so." And then he smiled at her, a slow easy smile. "But I wasn't an angel."

"Huh. Shocked."

He laughed and watched as her beautiful face turned pink.

"You know," she said tartly, "on second thought, I don't need you in the kitchen while I cook up your eggs. I can just go to YouTube."

❧

ERIKA MANAGED TO cook eggs and everything else Billy wanted. The bacon was burnt, the eggs were a hard dark yellow on the bottom, and the toast was cold, but it was food and after getting one of the bottles of hot sauce from his refrigerator and liberally dousing his plate, he ate every bite.

After breakfast, Billy told her to get to work, that he had Beck and she wasn't to worry about a thing. Erika glanced from Billy's sling to his stiff posture, aware that he could barely move without wincing, and she wanted to question if he could really be left alone with Beck, but she appreciated that he wanted to try.

"I'll just be in the next room," she said. "Come get me if you need—"

"I won't," he said, cutting her off. "I've got this."

She gave one last look at Beck propped up in his car seat on the coffee table facing his dad and smiled grimly. Beck would probably last ten minutes before he started crying. He didn't like being left in one position too long, but she didn't want to be a downer, not when Billy was trying to take on dad duties so that she could work.

In her room, she sat on her bed, laptop out, earbuds in to block out noise, and got down to work, aware that she didn't have all day. It took a few minutes before she remembered where she was, and what she needed to be doing, and then she was working, brain engaged, fingers flying on the laptop keyboard. It had been so long since she'd made headway, and it felt good to be productive, detached from the domestic worries, and free to just sink back into her writing.

She didn't know how long she'd been at work when she saw black sweatpants in her peripheral vision. Billy was standing next to the bed and she lifted her head, removed her ear pods.

"I can't get his diaper back on," Billy said. "My fault for trying to change him on the couch."

"Where is he now?"

"On the couch."

"Oh, Billy, he could roll off," she said, jumping to her

feet.

"I blocked him in," he answered, following her out of the bedroom.

In the living room she discovered that Billy really had blocked him in. Practically every pillow from the couch was positioned around him, forming a pillow corral. It worked for now while Beck was still so little, but in another month, Beck would be able to knock those around. She held her tongue though, and quickly lifted Beck, carrying him into her room to finish changing him.

Again, Billy followed her, watching as she rifled through a suitcase for diapers and a clean onesie since the other one was no longer wearable.

"You make that look so easy," Billy said from the doorway.

"I've had a month of practice," she answered, shooting him a quick smile. He looked ridiculously handsome this morning. Maybe it was the zipper halfway down on his sweatshirt, and the fact that his upper chest was all tantalizing bronzed skin and muscle, or maybe it was the shadow on his jaw that made him look rakish. "You'll be just as good, if not better, within a few weeks."

He didn't say anything for a moment. "He should have his own room, shouldn't he? With real furniture, not just a portable crib."

She snapped the onesie closed over Beck's diaper and gave his tummy a light pat. He gurgled up at her, his wide gummy smile delighting her as always. He was such a good baby, so sweet, so happy. "A changing table would be smart, too. It'd be easier for you to manage diaper changes."

"What else?"

"Maybe a high chair, since he'll be eating food soon. He could also sit in that and play with toys on the tray while you make yourself breakfast," she said, giving Billy an arched look as she lifted Beck from the bed and kissed his forehead.

Billy gave her a lazy smile. "I love your sense of humor."

Something in his eyes made her breath catch. The man had a ridiculous amount of charisma. She didn't want to be this attracted to him, and yet just looking at him made her feel a little weak in her knees, and a little light-headed. "So where do you want me to put him? On the floor for some tummy time, or in his car seat with the bar of toys in front of him?"

"The car seat would probably be easier. I don't think I can pick him up from the floor, not yet, at least."

"Maybe I should just hang out with you guys. You've only been out of the hospital for a day or so."

"You have work to do."

"I know, but I think it might be too soon to have you taking over." She saw his mouth open to protest and she hastily added, "You want to heal quickly, not prolong your recovery."

Billy's smile faded, and his gaze met hers and held. There was heat in his eyes, as well as that something that made her heart beat faster and her insides flutter. Was this the effect he had on all those other women? Blasted beast.

"You think of everyone but yourself," he said, his deep voice low, almost a growl.

A shiver raced through her, curiosity. Pleasure. "I'm less worried about me in the big picture, than I am of Beck—"

"You don't need to worry about Beck."

"But I do. Beck needs you. You have to stick around."

"Of course I'm sticking around."

"Not if you rush back into competing before you're ready. Not if you keep risking life and limb."

※

HE SAID NOTHING, but he did step back as she exited the room.

Erika faced him in the hallway. "What do you intend to do after you're done competing on the rodeo circuit?"

"Not even thinking that far ahead, as I have a good fifteen years or more of competition in me."

"Fifteen years?"

He tried to shrug but ended up wincing. "I love what I do."

Erika's temper stirred. He could be such a blockhead sometimes. "Is it realistic to think you can compete that long? I heard Sam talking about all of his injuries. Sounds like he's pretty banged up."

"Sam's had a lot more injuries than me—"

"You just had a big one."

"And I love competing more than he does," he retorted, ignoring her interruption. "There are other things Sam wants to do, like ranching, for example. But I'm not excited about ranching. I bought property without a lot of acreage because I don't want to spend the rest of my life doing what I did as a kid. I love what I'm doing now. If I could, I'd do it forever."

"That's a lot of travel. Almost a year of travel."

His jaw hardened. "That's what I like." His voice had grown flinty as well. "I enjoy being out on the road. I enjoy the camaraderie of other cowboys."

"And girls," she muttered.

"Oh yeah," he agreed, with a provocative smile. "Can't forget the girls."

Erika glowered, so over him. "I'm going to take Beck for a walk," she said curtly. "You're not invited."

They got through the rest of the day with minimal conversation. Billy slept much of the afternoon, and when Beck napped, Erika worked on her dissertation. Beck took a long nap today and she was able to get some solid work done, and still have time for a long hot bath in the tub in the guest bathroom.

Dinner was provided for them that night by a kind neighbor who had left the spaghetti and meatballs, garlic bread, and salad on the doorstep. It was all still warm and so nothing needed to be heated.

Billy had been the one to let her know that dinner was on the front doormat, and she just nodded and brought everything in.

She was still annoyed with him, and he seemed just as annoyed with her.

Good. The mutual frustration should help her cope with the lust feelings, effectively dousing some of his potent charm.

After dinner, Billy did his best to clean up using just his right hand, without bending too much. She let him clean up, too. If he was as tough as he said, and that enamored with his sport, then he could suffer through the minimal dishes.

She was sitting on the couch with Beck, giving Beck a last bottle for the night, when Billy asked if she'd like a cup of tea or anything.

It was the first time they'd spoken since she'd served dinner. "I'd love a cup," she said, as the evenings in Utah always grew cool. "As long as it's herbal, or decaf."

He brought her a mug of tea, the mug featuring a cowboy with the words, WORLD'S HOTTEST COWBOY, and she looked up at him, eyebrow arched. "Really?"

He smiled that slow, wicked, sexier-than-sin smile of his. "Just wanted to remind you."

Erika laughed. She couldn't help it. "You're impossible."

"Thank you."

"Ahem. That's not a compliment."

He eased into his armchair. "You know, my mom always

used to say the same thing."

"About being impossible?"

"But I think she secretly liked it. I was the one who made her smile. Mom has a tendency to be serious. It gave me pleasure knowing I could get her to laugh when no one else could. Laughter's important."

"It is important." Erika drew the bottle from Beck's lips and set it down. "You are important. You want to live a long life, just like your granddad. You want to be here for Beck's kids one day. That won't happen if you get gored or rolled on too many times."

"I appreciate your concern," he answered. "I'm being sincere, too. It's nice to know you care."

"I'm thinking of Beck."

"You can like me a little bit, Erika. It's okay."

❦

BILLY WATCHED AS soft pink color stained her cheeks, and she bit down into her lower lip, working it over as she did whenever she was nervous.

He wanted to be the one sucking on that lip. He wanted to feel her pressed against him. He'd wondered how she'd react if he brushed his lips across the curve of her cheek and the soft bow of her upper lip.

He'd liked the way her brow creased ever so slightly as if she didn't quite know what to do with him. He liked the uncertainty in her eyes that always reminded him of green turquoise. She had little flecks of gold and black against the green, the gold darker than her honey hair and arched eyebrows.

There was no doubt Erika was beautiful and smart and way too good for him, but every woman needed affection and it crossed his mind that it might have been a long time since she'd been shown affection. Since she'd been thoroughly, and properly, kissed. Loved.

Maybe it was a good thing he was still so broken and sore, because it limited his ability to move, severely curtailing his seduction skills. If he was going to take her to his bed, he'd do it properly, not half-assed. She needed hours of foreplay, and that required skill, and mobility. At least he had a goal, besides getting back to work.

"I do like you," she said crisply. "I wouldn't be here if I didn't."

"I thought you were here for Beck."

"That goes without saying. But I can care about you, too. Just because I want the best for you doesn't mean I want to be your next buckle bunny."

He grinned at her reference to the groupies and girls that hung around the rodeos, craving attention from the professional cowboys. "So glad we cleared that up. I might have gotten confused."

※

ERIKA SLEPT RESTLESSLY, dreaming of Billy, not sweet

dreams, either, but provocative dreams of him and her, dreams where he was kissing her and driving her crazy.

She woke up feeling a little besotted.

She hated it. She hated spending so much time thinking about Billy... his body, his face, his hands, his mouth. It didn't matter how he kissed, because she wasn't going to kiss him. It didn't matter if he looked hot. She wasn't going to touch him. It didn't matter if he'd woken her libido that had been dormant for years. She wasn't going to get laid.

She had to focus on why she was here, and then how she was going to shift gears, when it was time to shift gears.

And maybe that was the hardest part of all, thinking about leaving.

She didn't want to picture that day, or how it would feel to go, leaving Beck and Billy behind. Nothing inside of her found joy, or peace, in the prospect, and so she pushed it from her mind and left her bed to get her day started.

Just like yesterday, she helped Billy with his bandages and sling. Just like yesterday, she made him eggs—slightly less brown on the bottom, but this time the top layer looked weirdly wet—but he just covered it all in his Tapatio sauce and ate every bite.

Midmorning, she gave Beck another bottle and then after he fell asleep in her arms, she laid him in his travel crib and darkened the blinds and quietly shut the bedroom door. Not even five minutes later the doorbell rang, and she went to the front door and found two enormous boxes on the doorstep.

She shouted a thank you to the back of the departing driver, but the driver shouted back that he had more, quite a bit more. It actually took the driver four trips in all to deliver everything to the porch, and once he was gone, Erika stared at the mountain of cardboard boxes in dismay. How on earth was all of that to get into the house… and once there, where would it go?

Billy appeared then, cell phone in hand. "Did you call me?"

"No, I was thanking the driver." She nodded to the boxes. "Looks like it's Christmas."

"Oh good. Beck's things," he said, before lifting the phone back to his ear and saying to whomever was on the other line that he needed to go.

Once the phone was back in the front pocket of Billy's sweatpants, Erika asked him what he'd been buying. A complete nursery?

"Pretty much," Billy said. "This is his home. He should have his own room here, with toys and all the usual baby things."

"When did you order this?"

"Yesterday."

"And it's here today?"

"Anything can be rushed."

"That would cost a fortune."

He didn't seem concerned. "I have money. Why not spend it on my son?"

"True," she agreed.

"Besides, the furniture, there should be a swing for him. A standing saucer. And hopefully a bar with dangle toys so he can lie beneath them and reach for things."

How did he know about all these things? When had he done the research? "What didn't you buy?"

"There were a few things I left in the shopping cart. No need to overwhelm the little guy yet."

Her lips twitched. "You're becoming quite the expert."

"I can't just watch TV all day."

"No, you can't. Pretty soon you'll be schooling me."

"I do some have thoughts, actually, but this might not be the time." He closed the front door, blocking the view of the huge boxes. "We can talk about it later tonight—"

"Talk about what?"

"I just wondered if it was time to start him on some solid foods. He's only five months, but he can hold his head up just fine, and he wants to eat. When I take a bite, he leans forward and opens his mouth."

"I'd read somewhere that six months is better."

"Either way, we'll start with cereal, and then in a month or two introduce fruits, vegetables, yogurt. Cereal will fill him up better than just milk. He'll probably take better naps, too, with a full belly."

Erika's head was spinning. These were all things she'd wanted to bring up to Billy, expecting she'd have to do a fair amount of educating him, but instead, he'd brought her up to speed, and he'd executed the plan. "I can look for infant cereal when I go shopping this weekend."

"I can drive you to Bryce. We'll all go."

"You think it's a good idea to drive?"

"I'm right-handed. My truck is an automatic."

"I don't want you to hurt."

"I'll be fine."

"So, what do we do with all those boxes out there? From the looks of it, almost everything will need to be put together."

"I'll handle that. Don't worry about a thing."

"Are you going to do all of that with just one hand, too?"

"No. But I know someone who can get it done for us without too much effort."

Not even fifteen minutes later there was a knock on the front door. Erika answered, opening the door to discover a young cowboy on the front porch.

"Mr. Wyatt sent me a text; said he needed some help." The young cowboy couldn't have been much older than twenty or twenty-one. He swept off his hat revealing dark hair and a dusting of freckles across his cheekbones. "I'm Brad Mott, but everyone calls me Boom."

"Boom?" she repeated.

He nodded, grinned. "When I was little, I liked to crash things, and when I did, I'd go boom." His grin widened. "I guess the name stuck."

"Well, Boom, I'm Erika Baylor," she said extending her

hand. "Nice to meet you. I'll take you to Billy."

It took Boom most of the afternoon to get the crib and dresser put together, with Billy reading instructions, and holding pieces that he could, and then they tackled the high chair and by the time that was done Boom had to get home to feed the livestock.

Erika asked Billy about Boom after he was gone. "I take it, he's a neighbor?"

"Lives just a couple miles down the road. His folks' property butts up against mine. He's helped me for a couple of years now, keeping an eye on things when I'm not here, and helping me with the odd job when I am home."

"So, he's not a rodeo cowboy?"

"He's just your hardworking, salt of the earth cowboy. He's the real deal."

She smiled. "I like him. He's a nice guy."

"He's saving up to get married—"

"What? He's so young!"

"Almost twenty—"

"Even younger than I thought."

"Boom and his girlfriend have been serious for a couple years. I've been thinking of hiring him on full-time. It'd give him steady income and Ellen would be happy knowing he's got a good job close to home."

"Is Ellen his girlfriend?"

"His mom. She used to be an ER nurse, but the local hospital closed and she didn't want to be driving an hour to get to work."

"You know your neighbors pretty well."

"I've lived here a few years now. We're all pretty isolated. It's important to know who's near you in case something happens."

The next day, Billy oversaw the setup of Beck's room, by directing Boom to place the crib just so, and then the small dresser which also served as a changing table against the opposite wall. He carefully crouched down, keeping his torso upright as he plugged the small bucking horse night-light in, and then rose, his gaze sweeping the room, clearly pleased with what he saw. "It looks good," he said, glancing at Erika who'd been watching from the doorway. "What do you think?"

"I think it looks great. We'll fill the top dresser drawer with diapers when we buy them, and the next drawer with Beck's clothes when we've washed them." She frowned. "Speaking of which, I should do that today. I haven't done laundry in ages, not since our second day in Boise when I used the motel's laundry room."

Boom stayed for lunch—he'd brought the lunch, actually, thick roast beef and cheddar sandwiches on freshly baked bread—and during lunch, he and Billy discussed farm things and the horses and Erika's mind drifted, as she considered her work. She really didn't feel inspired. There was nothing in her that wanted to go to her room and be alone for hours. She'd always thought of herself as an introvert, preferring her own company over others, but being alone wasn't appealing, not when fascinating, larger-than-life Billy Wyatt was in the next room.

She did get a little work done later, not enough to brag about, but in her room, she could at least pretend to be focused. Productive.

But a half hour into revising a section of her paper, she got a calendar reminder that rent was past due.

It was already early April.

Erika had never missed her rent before and couldn't believe she'd forgotten it. How many other things was she forgetting? But life in Riverside was a world away from Billy's cozy Utah cabin, and the longer she was here, the more comfortable she became. Her new daily routine included lots of teasing and banter, never mind breakfast, lunch, and dinner with Billy. She liked helping him get bandaged up, liked helping him dress, liked the shivery sensation she got when standing close to him, her lips just inches from the taut planes of his broad chest.

She closed the laptop and lay back on her bed, staring up at the beams in the ceiling, and the slow whirl of the rustic fan that kept the air moving.

How much longer would she stay here? Billy ought to have use of both arms soon, she thought, as well as the ability to lift and carry Beck without pain in his ribs. That would be what... a month? Two? Either way, the time would pass quickly, and that was both good and bad, because the passage of time brought her closer and closer to her dissertation's due date. She'd done almost nothing in the past six weeks. She'd regret her lack of focus later. But now, now she was needed, and wanted, and it was the best feeling.

Erika left her room and went to the living room where Beck was swinging away in his swing, while Billy watched TV. She walked past the basket of toys in the corner—a soft chunky truck, a fabric book, a teething ring that looked like a black and white cow—and thought yet again how lucky Beck was. Billy was going to be a great dad.

Her heart suddenly ached. Billy and his boy. They'd make a great team.

Chapter Eight

Billy woke to the sound of soft fussing from Beck's room, the morning cry that Billy had come to identify as *hello, I'm awake*. Billy looked at the time. It was almost five thirty. Still dark out. But Beck didn't seem to mind that the world was sleeping, he was ready to get up. Granddad was the same. Always awake before dawn.

Billy left bed, left arm bent at the elbow and pressed to his side and went to Beck's room. He flipped on the little night-light and leaned over the crib. Beck was staring up at him with bright blue eyes, and the moment he spotted Billy, he gurgled and smiled, his wide irresistible smile. Billy's chest tightened, filled with love and a fierce, primitive desire to protect his baby from all dangers. He'd do anything for Beck, just as he'd do anything for his brothers.

Billy carefully scooped up Beck with his right arm, carrying him to the changing table to get a dry diaper on him. Beck kept his wiggling to a minimum, just kicking legs a little bit as Billy drew the pajamas back up and then zipped the zipper, keeping Beck snug.

Together, they headed toward the living room, passing

Erika's room. Her door was still closed. No light shone beneath the door. Billy hoped she was still sleeping as she tended to stay up late and wake early. She probably needed far more sleep than she was getting.

They continued on to the kitchen where Billy slid Beck into his high chair so that he could put on a pot of coffee and then, while that was brewing, he turned his focus to a bottle for Beck. Before giving his son the bottle, Billy turned on the heat, and then lit the gas in the fireplace in the living room, and then carried first the coffee to the living room, then Beck and the bottle.

Beck was impatient for the bottle and gurgled his displeasure that he was being kept waiting. "Patience, little man," Billy said, easing into his recliner. "You'll have your milk soon enough. Let me just have one sip of coffee, okay?"

Beck emptied his bottle in record time and Billy did his best to burp him, shifting the baby against his good shoulder and giving him firm pats on the back. Beck's hand reached up into Billy's hair, grabbing little tufts and giving them hard tugs.

Beck was a strong little thing and growing by the day. He'd filled out a lot—if that was possible, considering he was a little chunk of love to begin with. It crossed Billy's mind that maybe he should head back to Paradise Valley, spend a weekend with Mom and Granddad, and give them a chance to know his son better. He'd love to show Erika around Marietta, too. It was a great Western town, filled with lots of historical buildings and some new great restaurants. And then there was Grey's Saloon, his favorite place for a beer. Maybe Joe and Sophie could watch Beck for an hour or two while Billy took Erika to Grey's. Did Erika even drink beer? He was fairly confident she didn't play pool.

And then he stopped himself.

There was no reason to take Erika to Montana, no reason to show her around. They weren't in a relationship, and she wasn't going to be an integral part of his life much longer. She was Beck's aunt, or second cousin, or something along those lines, but he didn't know how much of a relationship Erika and Beck would have once she returned to California. Billy wasn't the type to stay in touch with those outside his own family. He never did the chasing, either. If a girl wanted him, they came after him, not vice versa. He wouldn't hunt Erika down, not even when his travel took him to Southern California. Why invite trouble? And Erika was trouble. She was beautiful, desirable, and not available.

She'd never be available.

She was Beck's mother's family and he wasn't about to hurt family, and he did hurt women. He disappointed them constantly. So no, Erika wouldn't go with him. Which made him wonder, when would she go?

Which made his gut cramp because Beck would miss her something awful. Beck loved her and was attached to her and his little face lit up every time she entered the room. When he hadn't seen her for a while he got fussy and restless, clearly needing to be back in her arms.

Billy dreaded the day Beck had to get used to life without her. Beck would grieve. He'd cry. He'd miss her.

But eventually he'd forget. Eventually he'd move on. He didn't have a choice. That was just how life worked.

※

ERIKA STRETCHED, ENJOYING soft sheets and warmth of the bed. She'd had such a good night sleep. She slowly opened her eyes, relaxed, content, wondering what time it was. Sunlight peeked around the blinds in her room. The clock read seven thirty. Erika sat up, panicked.

Beck.

Billy.

Throwing the covers back, she scrambled out of bed, threw on a sweatshirt and raced from her room. Beck's door was open and his crib empty. She headed toward the living room and heard Billy's voice. He was talking to someone, probably on the phone. But, arriving in the living room, she discovered he wasn't on the phone. He was having a very long, one-sided conversation with his son.

Her lips curved, and she smiled, pleased. It was about time Billy started having father-son conversations.

Billy looked up and spotted her. "How did you sleep?"

"So good," she answered, going to the fireplace to warm herself. This past week the mornings had been really cold, even as the afternoons warmed up. "Have you two been up long?"

"Since five thirty."

"Oh no. I didn't hear him crying."

"He wasn't fussing too much. Just saying hello. He was ready to get up."

"He's an early bird."

"Granddad always was. I never liked those early morning hours, especially when you had to go to the barn and do chores." Billy nodded to the kitchen. "Coffee's made, but you might want to put on a fresh pot. That's been sitting for a couple hours."

"As long as it's hot, I'm good." She headed to the kitchen, glanced out the window over the sink. Blue, blue sky and a golden sun. It was going to be a gorgeous day. She filled her cup, added a splash of cream and one artificial sugar before returning to the living room.

"Want me to take him?" she asked Billy, indicating Beck.

Billy glanced down at Beck who was starting to look sleepy. "Maybe in a minute. He's comfortable right now."

"He does look very relaxed," she agreed, settling into the corner of the couch near Billy's chair. "What's your plan for the day?"

"Besides showering, dressing, and getting in your way?"

She smiled crookedly. "You're not in my way. I'm probably in your way, keeping you from doing whatever it is you usually do when you're here."

"Nope. For one, I'm not here all that often, just a couple

of times a month at the most. And when I am, I'm usually doing laundry and washing the truck and trailer and getting ready for my next road trip."

"No local girls to keep you company?"

"This is a bachelor pad. No women invited."

"Seriously?"

"You're the first woman that's been here."

"I find that hard to believe."

He gave her a long, unsmiling look. "I'm not a man whore, despite what you think of me—"

"I've never said that."

"You didn't have to. It's implied in everything you say or do."

"I don't—"

"No, you do," he interrupted firmly, but not unkindly. "Just because I haven't fallen in love and settled down yet, doesn't mean I view women as tissue—something to be used and discarded. I like women. I respect women. I'm not an asshole. I'm sorry I hurt April. I'm sorry she didn't feel comfortable coming to me and telling me she was pregnant, because I wouldn't have turned her away. I wouldn't have told her it was her problem. I would have been a man and done the right thing."

That was a long speech coming from Billy. Erika wasn't sure she'd ever heard him put so many sentences together at one time. "I'm sorry if I offended you."

"I've always taken my responsibilities seriously."

She rubbed her thumb along the rim of the warm mug. "Would you have married her?"

His features hardened, expression grim. "If that's what she'd wanted."

"Even though you didn't love her?"

"Love might have grown over time." He shrugged, his right shoulder twisting. "And if not, hopefully friendship would have been there."

Erika hated the idea of April and Billy married. It was wrong of her, but it made her jealous, and vaguely sick. "I didn't expect that from you."

He didn't reply and she dropped her gaze back to her mug. "And I imagine, April didn't, either," Erika added unsteadily.

"She should have come to me. I had a right to know that I'd created a child. I understand she was carrying it, but that it took two to make Beck, and I should have been involved from the beginning."

"I don't know what she was thinking. I didn't even know Beck existed. She'd kept his birth from me."

"Who knew then?"

"Her mom, my aunt. I don't think my aunt even told anyone else. She was ashamed that April was a single mom. It wasn't okay, not in our family."

"I thought her mom was hooking up with different guys."

"She went back to the church a couple years ago. She's

more devout than even her parents were."

"Nothing like a reformed sinner."

Erika knew it. Her mom had begun to spend more time with her aunt Sara. She was even dating someone in the Fundamentalist church. "Sometimes very religious families are the least loving of all," she said, rising from the couch and pacing to the set of French doors with the view of the valley and the distant rugged red rocks. "You'd think my mom and aunt would have compassion for April, but no, she'd chosen a heathen lifestyle."

"I'm not a fan of formal religion for that very reason. I think there should be a lot more compassion and forgiveness. People need love. I didn't attend a lot of church when I was a boy, but Granddad read the bible to us every night and we always said grace and prayers. Granddad said the most important thing we could do was treat people well and to love. Love God, love your family, love your neighbor."

She turned and looked at him. "And your enemy?"

"Probably love your enemy most of all, but that's not as easy."

"Which is why it probably needs to be done."

"Agreed." He looked at her a long moment, expression serious. "Are you okay?"

"Yes. Why?"

"You seem… sad. Upset."

"Now who is the therapist?" she flashed, forcing a light smile. "Would you like breakfast? I'm ready to try fried eggs, if you want them."

"I'd love a shower first."

"I'll take Beck, you shower, and then I'll make breakfast."

"Sounds like a plan."

She crossed to him and reached down for Beck who'd just drifted off. As she leaned over to pick him up her gaze met Billy's and held. They were just inches apart, so close she could feel his breath on her lips and see tiny silver bits in his blue irises. He was gorgeous from afar and heart stopping close. She wanted a kiss. Wanted his warmth. She saw the moment he registered her desire. His gaze darkened and smoldered. Her mouth dried and a shiver coursed through her. Why couldn't she kiss him?

Why couldn't she do what she'd been thinking about?

Her gaze dropped to his mouth. He had a perfect mouth, perfect lips.

"A kiss won't be enough," he said, his deep voice raspy, scratching across her senses as if she'd stroked sandpaper.

She looked back into his eyes. They glowed bright. "It would if it was a bad one," she whispered.

"It won't be bad. Nothing between us could ever be bad."

And just like that, a frisson of excitement shot through her, making her dizzy and breathless. "You know just what a woman likes to hear," she said, easing the baby from his arms, and taking several steps back.

Some of the fire faded from his eyes. "This isn't about anyone else. This is about me and you."

"But we can't have a me and you, can we?" She struggled to keep her tone even, pleasant. "It'd be just sex."

"Sex is wonderful."

She focused on slipping Beck into his new reclining bouncy seat, and then strapped the little belt so he'd be secure. She adjusted the belt a little bit more to keep from meeting Billy's eyes. "Sex makes cute little babies like this guy."

"If we did it, we'd use protection." Billy rose. "But we're not going to do it. We can't do it. It'd change everything, and that wouldn't be fair to Beck, or you."

She managed a jerky nod. "Thank you for keeping an eye on the big picture. I appreciate it."

"You know I find you incredibly attractive—"

"Let's not do this." She gave him a bright, fierce smile, one with lots of teeth. "We both know what's at stake, and we've both agreed it'd be a mistake. Now let me go sort out breakfast. And it might just have to be scrambled again today. I don't think I can handle trying anything new."

After making breakfast, eggs for both of them, Erika carried her plate into her bedroom and sat down on the bed to work and eat. For ten minutes, she struggled to focus on the screen but her mind was completely blank.

She felt angry. Embarrassed. Frustrated. Furious. That whole conversation had been miserable. Being told by Billy what they could, and couldn't do, ticked her off.

He made it sound like he was the wise one, the one with discipline and maturity. If he was so mature, why did he only want sexual relationships? Why didn't he want emotional connections? Why did he run away from anything that remotely resembled love?

If he was so wise, why was he attracted to her in the first place?

She wasn't his type. She didn't like cowboys. She hated the rodeo. She disagreed with most of the decisions he'd ever made in life. He was foolish and arrogant and stubborn and completely in denial when it came to his own mortality.

And yet she wanted to wrap her arms around him and hold him tight. She wanted to press her face to his chest and breathe him in and let his warmth sink into her. And maybe some of his courage and bravado. As well as his humor. She loved his laughter, and the way he smiled, and that little groove next to his mouth that deepened when he was holding back a smile.

She was crazy about him.

Crazy, stupid.

Blinking back tears, she left the bed, and carried her plate back to the kitchen. Billy was there, at the sink, doing dishes with one arm.

"I was going to do those later," she said.

"No biggie. It's my turn."

"I don't mind—"

"You're not a maid." He turned the water off, and faced her. "I do need to get you some money, though. You've spent weeks taking care of Beck, weeks where you can't work your other jobs."

"I don't want your money. He's my cousin."

"That was our deal."

"There was no deal, Billy. Beck needed me and I wasn't about to leave him, not until he'd formed a strong attachment to you."

"Has he?" Billy asked, his gaze narrowed.

"Are you asking my personal opinion or my professional opinion?"

"Has he bonded enough with me for him to not suffer when you leave?"

She winced. "I can't answer that."

"Why not?"

"Because—" She broke off, swallowed hard. "In general, babies less than six months old adjust better to a loss of a primary adult than babies who are older. As long as Beck's needs are met, he should ultimately thrive."

"Why was that so hard to say?"

She shrugged uncomfortably. "It'll be an adjustment though. Babies don't understand the concept of time, so he might be upset by my absence. Initially." She couldn't stand this conversation. She didn't even want to be in this house anymore. "I'm thinking of heading into town to go shopping. Need diapers, wipes, maybe a few outfits. Just something comfy for the day as he's getting big."

"We can go to Bryce."

"Sam had mentioned I'd find basics there." She hesitated. "But you don't have to go. Beck and I can make the drive together."

"You don't know your way."

"I have GPS on my phone."

"I'll drive you."

"Billy."

"Yes, Erika?"

She looked away, counted to ten. "Don't you think we need some time apart?"

"I think what we need is fresh air. We have cabin fever. And I have just the remedy for that."

She watched him turn the water back on and rinse the skillet he'd been washing earlier. "Where will we go?"

"You'll see," he answered, setting the skillet on the counter.

"How should I dress?"

"In clothes." He grinned. "Unless you'd rather not?"

"Are you having fun?"

"I am."

He was, too. She could hear it in his voice, see it in his eyes. He was in a good mood and enjoying teasing her. "I probably will wear clothes. It's a bit brisk out there."

"Alright then, since you're determined to wear clothes, put on something comfortable, something with layers, and shoes you can walk in."

Sounded like they'd be getting some exercise. Good. She needed it. "And Beck?"

"Layers for sure, but I'm not sure he's ready to do much walking."

"You haven't bought him cowboy boots yet? I'm shocked."

Billy's lips quirked and his blue eyes crinkled at the corners. "Who said I haven't bought him boots? Maybe you just haven't seen them."

They left the house twenty minutes later, with the baby carrier, a full diaper bag, and lots of formula.

Billy's window was halfway down and the air blew through the truck, crisp and invigorating. Even as dazzling spring sunshine blinded them, Erika didn't ask where they were going, content to let Billy drive, and he did, traveling the single lane highway through a narrow valley, next to a river that bordered pastures where herds of cattle and bison grazed. She leaned on her door, soaking up the scenery, thinking it was nice to be a passenger and just sit back and relax. Not that she could relax too long. After their drive, she had to get back to work. Needed to find a way to focus again.

The distant pink mountains grew more weathered and impressive as they approached. Gradually, the rugged pink stone turned into striking red rocks, reminding Erika of Thunder Mountain at Disneyland. The rock formations were stunning and she leaned out her window taking pictures of them, begging Billy to slow down so she could get yet another photo.

❦

BILLY WAS AMUSED by her enthusiasm. Over the years, he'd taken family and friends out to see Bryce, but his friends were unexpressive dudes who undoubtedly enjoyed the scenery but didn't communicate this awe and wonder. He rather liked her awe and wonder and slowed to a crawl at her request so she could snap a photo of the massive red rock they were about to drive through.

"What are you going to do with all these photos?" he asked.

She caught her hair in her hand to keep it from blowing everywhere, and yet long golden tendrils still danced around her face, clinging to her lashes. "Look at them. Remember how beautiful it is."

He shot her an appreciative glance. She was beautiful. A fresh, natural beauty. "Wait until you see Bryce Canyon. You'll love it. We're going to do an easy trail, nothing too demanding since you'll have Beck and I have myself."

She laughed, the sound bubbly and buoyant. "I'd rather carry Beck than you," she said. "You'd be a smidge too heavy."

He looked at her again, thinking she was glowing, her eyes—that unusual turquoise blue green—bright, her lips curved. She reminded him of a cowgirl. Strong, smart, full of heart. Erika had a country vibe, even if she didn't know it.

She was everything he liked, everything he could want in a woman. Without wanting to, he'd developed feelings for her. She was on his mind more often than not lately. Unfortunately, what he wanted to do with her was more wicked than sweet. He wanted her and being alone with her in the house only made the desire stronger.

He liked her in his house, though, and didn't want to think about the day she wouldn't be there anymore.

She'd made his place cozy. Homey. And it had never been that before. It was a cabin. Practical. Rustic. Undemanding. It was always there when he needed it and nobody fussed when he left.

But it felt different with a baby and a woman in it. It was as if it had become a family home and it was strange and yet rather wonderful at the same time. He hadn't thought he'd want, or need, a homey place, but he'd grown accustomed to having company. He liked waking up and finding Erika in the kitchen, or seeing her curled up in a chair, reading. He liked the way she'd look up at him and smile. He liked the sound of her voice and the way she sang even though she didn't carry a tune, and somehow the fact that she liked to sing and hum, even though she wasn't a talented singer, made him enjoy it even more. She wasn't perfect, and she wasn't pretending to be perfect. She was just herself, and that was what made her special. She was who she was, and in his mind, she was exactly right, and exactly who she was meant to be.

"How are you coming with your dissertation?" he asked, drawing his wallet from his back pocket and he approached the park entrance. "Getting all that writing down?"

She hesitated. "I guess."

He flashed his annual park membership card at the park ranger and was waved in. "That doesn't sound very convincing."

"I'm making some progress. Maybe not quite as much as I'd hoped."

"I can hire a sitter. Boom's mom, Ellen, would love regular work."

"That just doesn't seem right."

"What doesn't seem right is you not completing something you've spent years working on."

"I'm not giving up on it, but it doesn't feel as important as everything else happening right now."

He wasn't that easily placated. "But it is important. It's incredibly important. This is your degree, your career—"

"Yes," she interrupted with a sigh. "It is. It's very important. But let's not think about it today. It just feels so good to be out. I am loving all this Utah scenery. It feels like we're having an adventure—" She broke off and flashed him another one of her quick smiles that warmed her eyes and made her generous lips curve, revealing her small, straight white teeth.

He felt a tug in his chest, gratitude and something else, because when Erika smiled, she was radiant. There was no woman more beautiful than her.

"I love adventures," she added. "Don't you?"

He felt that tug in his chest again. It was such an inexplicable emotion. Not exactly good, but not exactly bad. Unsettling was more like it. "I like my adventures, too," he said pulling into a parking lot that was half empty. Easter was late this year, practically the last week of April, and by then there would be more tourists, but it was still early in the season and they'd have most of the park trails to themselves. "That's why I love being on the pro circuit. Every week, every rodeo is a new adventure."

"I think your idea of an adventure and mine are very different." She gave a little sniff, her nose in the air. "In my adventures, I don't almost die."

He laughed, because she made him laugh. He didn't think he'd ever met a woman so opposite of him in every way, but their differences didn't bother him. If anything, he liked it. He liked her, more than he should. Billy turned off the engine and faced her. "I have no death wish. I'm not riding bulls and broncs because I don't have other choices. I'm doing it because I'm good at it. I like it, and I like that I can make a lot of money doing it."

"I've heard you say that a couple of times, and I see what you've been able to do with your earnings, or whatever you call it in cowboy speak, but at some point, when is it enough? Can't you invest what you've already earned and find something less dangerous to do?"

"I could, but I like what I do. I love what I do. And I know you don't like it but you don't have to. That's okay. Being a cowboy is my thing." He opened his door then, ready to get out and move, as well as move on from this topic. He knew how she felt about his career, but it was his career. She had her path. He had his. And sometimes the differences between them were charming, but other times, like now when they were discussing his passion, her opinion aggravated him. He was a man that went by the motto, live and let live. It was a good motto, one his grandfather had ascribed to, and it had seen Billy through some challenging situations.

Erika quickly checked Beck's diaper—he was wet—so she did a fast diaper change on the passenger seat of the truck and then put on the baby carrier and strapped him in on her chest.

They set off on a dirt trail and moments later came to the edge of a cliff with the most stunning view of pink and crimson rock formations. The entire valley stretched before them, all chiseled pink and red, studded with magnificent pink rocks.

"Beautiful," she whispered.

"Bryce Amphitheater," he said, before pointing with his right arm to the unusual spire rock formations. "And those are hoodoos."

"Hoodoos?" she repeated, and just saying the word made her smile.

"It is a great word, isn't it? You should see the amphitheater at sunrise or sunset. That's when you get all the photographers out, trying to capture the perfect shot."

"Does it get crowded here?"

"Yes, but nothing like Zion, southwest of here. Zion draws a lot more people, which is why I avoid it, but one day you should see it."

"I had no idea Utah was so beautiful."

"There's so much to see in this part of the state. Grand Staircase, Escalante, Capitol Reef, the little historic towns Fruita, and Torrey. I never have enough time to just explore, but that's the plan for one of these days."

"I've spent so much time on a university campus I sometimes forget there's a big world out there just waiting to be discovered."

"Feel like walking?"

"Absolutely."

THEY'D WALKED DOWN a slope for twenty minutes, passing gnarled trees and through walls and arches of stunning pink stone. Beck was so light he was easy to carry, and the fresh air and views, so stunning at every turn, made Erika feel as if she was walking in an enchanted wonderland. They paused midway down the mountain to soak it up and let Erika take some more photos.

But Erika wasn't ready to start walking again. She'd been feeling guilty ever since they parked and it was time she got it off her chest. "I'm sorry if I sound so negative about your career. I don't mean to be—" She broke off, drew a breath, and tried again. "It's none of my business, what you do, but I just… care… about you. I care about you a lot, and I'd hate for anything to happen to you. You're such a good person, a really wonderful person, I just want you to stay safe, and be here fifty years from now."

Billy didn't immediately answer. "I don't know who I would be without the rodeo. It's who I am. It's what defines me."

"That's not really true, you know," Erika said quietly, giving Beck's back a little rub through the soft fabric of the navy carrier. "You would still be you. Smart, funny, kind, courageous, Billy Wyatt."

He said nothing. She could see he was troubled.

"If I'd met you apart from the rodeo," she added, "and I just met you and I knew nothing about your fame or success, I'd think you were intriguing. The rodeo doesn't make you interesting, *you* make the rodeo interesting."

He glanced down at her, expression shuttered. "That's nice of you."

"I'm being sincere. You're special, Billy." She swallowed hard, her face warm. Had she said too much? She probably had, but she still couldn't stop talking. More words tumbled from her mouth. "You don't have to say anything. I just needed you to know I'm sorry for criticizing. I shouldn't be negative. I'll just say, please be careful, Billy Wyatt, because you mean a lot to a lot of people."

For a moment, silence stretched, a long humming silence filled with things they avoided saying. He finally broke the silence. "Does that include you?"

Her cheeks grew warmer. Her voice dropped lower. "Yes."

"You'd miss me if I wasn't around?"

Her eyes stung. An uncomfortable lump filled her throat. "I think it'd break my heart."

He reached out, lightly stroked her cheek with the pad of his thumb. "Don't want to do that."

Chapter Nine

SHE DIDN'T KNOW which made her feel more, his touch, or his words. Combined, they made the ache in her chest grow, filling her with tenderness and pain.

What she felt for him wasn't infatuation. What she felt went so much deeper than that. She wanted what was best for him. She wanted him safe. She wanted him to live a long, happy life.

He gently stroked her cheek again, a sweeping caress from the corner of her mouth, up over her cheekbone, and then back again. "Why do you look so sad?"

"You make me feel, and it's not always comfortable," she said.

His hand fell away. "Life's not always comfortable."

"No," she agreed huskily, looking away, trying to pull herself together.

She was hooked on him. She'd fallen in love with him. She didn't know why, because he wasn't practical, or safe, and she was risk-adverse, but now that he was in her heart, she didn't know how to get him out.

"I don't have a death wish, Erika," he said after a moment. "I'd like to end up like Granddad, eighty-nine years old and in better shape than men half his age."

"That's a goal I can relate to, as I'd like to see you loved, the way your grandfather is loved by all of you. You, Beck, Beck's kids."

"You're awfully determined to give me a family."

"You already have a family, a big family. The family you were born into, and now the family you're creating. Beck is just the first of your children. I'm sure there will be more."

"You're also determined to make me settle down."

"You're already somewhat settled. You have a great home. You have a son. You have what most men would love to have."

"Not women?" he countered. "You don't want a home, and family?"

"Of course I do, down the road, if I meet the right person—"

"You make that sound as if that's going to be a challenge."

"I'm not for everybody. And honestly, not everyone's for me."

"What do you want? From a man?"

His voice had dropped, and firmed, and she looked away from him, to gaze out over the dramatic pink rocks. "I want him to love me."

"That's a given," Billy said.

"No, it's not. My mom and dad didn't have much love

between them, and even less tolerance. They picked at each other constantly. It was excruciating."

"You're not them. You won't make the same choices, or the same mistakes."

"I'm afraid, though. Afraid that maybe—" She broke off, shook her head.

"Maybe what?" he persisted.

She bit the inside of her cheek, considered the men she'd dated, remembered who they'd been and how incredibly unsatisfying the relationships had been. "Maybe I'm unlovable."

"Bullshit."

She couldn't look at him. "I think I might need too much."

"Of what?"

"Hugs. Love. Words of affection." She forced herself to look up, her gaze meeting his. "I think I'm going to need too much reassurance, and it won't be an easy thing for a man. Men don't like needy women."

He let out a rough laugh. "You're the least needy woman I know."

"Maybe it's because you don't know me."

"So what are you hiding from me?"

It was her turn to laugh, a very uncomfortable laugh. "What am I not hiding?"

"Hit me with one thing."

She squinted against the bright warm sun, thinking. She

wasn't even sure where to begin. "I'd rather hang out with you and Beck than sit in my room and do my dissertation."

"How is that a bad thing? I wouldn't enjoy spending a year or more writing a paper. I wouldn't enjoy spending a day writing a paper."

"Yes, but I've lost all interest in my dissertation. I don't seem to care about the future anymore." She turned and looked at him again, her gaze sweeping his impossibly handsome face. "I've lived my life by a list of goals and suddenly those goals seem less important than just being happy now."

"Are you happy?"

"These past few weeks have been the happiest of my life." She shrugged. "And I worry that all my goals were a distraction to keep me from realizing how unhappy I was."

"Okay, slow down. You're upset with yourself for feeling good?"

"I'm feeling so good that I don't want to work."

"That's not abnormal, Erika." He smiled at her, a rather tender, amused smile. "You might need to counsel yourself, because you're not saying anything shocking. You're not saying anything weird, or deviant. You just happen to be aware of your weaknesses."

She had nothing to say to this. She was almost embarrassed they were having this long conversation about her issues. She preferred it when they were discussing him and his.

"No one is productive all the time," he added. "No one is at their best all of the time. We have highs and lows, and you're going to have lows. You just have to push through, not give up, and not give up on your dissertation. You've worked far too hard to lose focus now. What can I do to make things easier? Hire Ellen? Ask her to do some cooking for us while caring for Beck? Do I need a housekeeper? What would allow you to start making progress again?"

She couldn't tell him that she didn't want to write and work, that she just wanted to be with him, but it sounded pathetic even to herself. "Childcare would help. Some meals would be nice. I'm not adept in the kitchen—"

"You're better than you were."

She smiled crookedly. "Thank you. I think."

"What else is worrying you? Tell me. Let me help if I can."

"Money." Her voice cracked. "I need to bring in some money again. It's going to be tough making my rent payment for June if I don't get my act together."

"I'll cover your rent—"

"No."

"Why not? You've given up your life for Beck, and he's my son. Let me help you."

"Because Beck has been a gift, and a joy. I don't want to take money from you for doing something I've loved."

"Why is it okay for you to take care of Beck, but I can't help take care of you?"

Heat rushed through her again, as well as a wash of shame. "I take care of Beck because he's a baby. I'm not an infant. You shouldn't have to take care of me. I should be able to take care of myself."

"You've helped take care of me since I was hurt, and I'm not an infant."

"It's different. You were injured. You had serious injuries, too—"

"I'm beginning to understand. Everyone else can be human but not you. You're superhuman, and therefore, should be perfect."

Annoyed, she shot him a hard, narrowed glance. "No."

"If you feel needy, it's because you think it's somehow wrong to have needs, and I don't know what your psychology experts say about that, but I was raised to think that it's okay to have needs, and it's okay to struggle, and it's okay to ask for help."

Temper flaring, Erika faced him, her hands rubbing Beck's back as if to soothe him when in reality she was trying to calm herself. "If you're such an expert, why don't you want more for yourself? Why do you pursue women who are satisfied with just your body, and don't want more of you? Why want women who are willing to accept your rules? Why not let yourself be challenged by a woman who wants the best from you, not just sex from you?"

He lifted a brow. "How long have you been holding that in?"

"I'm serious! Why don't you want to be loved? Why don't you want something permanent? What has made you afraid of love?"

"Not afraid of love," he answered promptly. "I just don't love."

"You love your brothers, and your mom—"

"And Granddad," he agreed.

"So you love."

"But I don't *fall* in love. I have *never* fallen in love. There has never been that deep connection, or earth-shattering emotion and attachment that makes me think this is something I want forever, that without this person, I don't want to live—"

"I don't know that that is love. That's storybook stuff, romance novels and Disney movies. Love is an attachment. That's exactly what love is."

"But I don't feel it, and as I don't enjoy hurting people, I discourage women from getting attached to me. Thus, hooking up works for me. I'm not causing anyone pain. I'm not disappointing anyone—"

"Just selling yourself short."

"*How?*"

"Because you can't become attached if you never spend time with anyone. You won't ever feel connected if you don't invest in someone. Love grows over time. Again, it's not the fairy tale where you lock eyes across the room and suddenly fall in love. Love is a muscle. The more you use it, the stronger it is." She looked down at the top of Beck's cap covering his head. "You didn't have any feelings for Beck when you first met him, but now you do."

"He's my son."

"But it's not just head knowledge. You're connected now because you're protective of him. You're bonding by being together. You feel love in part because you've taken care of him, and you want him safe. Happy. That bond didn't happen in one day, either. It's been a progression—"

"Okay, Dr. Baylor, you've made your point. Love takes time, needs to grow, it's more organic that the media portrays. Is that it?"

She nodded.

"Great. I'll keep an open mind next time I meet a woman in a bar—"

"Billy."

"What? That's what you're saying, isn't it?"

"You're being deliberately obtuse."

"I do love it when you use big words."

"Now you're just trying to push my buttons."

"Maybe." He glanced out over the Bryce canyon and then up toward the slope they'd walked down. "I suggest we head back up. Beck's going to get hungry and I don't think I can handle any more talking without lunch."

She nodded, feeling deflated, as well as somewhat defeated. Why was she so determined to give him 'advice,' especially when it came to women?

Why was she determined to share so much? Lecture so much?

What did she think she was going to do, change him and make him the man she wanted him to be? A man that would cheerfully retire from the rodeo, and get a nice, safe day job, and be the partner she wanted him to be?

That wasn't Billy, and it wasn't fair to try to make him over into the man she wanted. He was a good person, a wonderful person, the way he was. Women loved who he was. He loved who he was. And if he was happy with his world, and his choices, maybe she needed to stop weighing in.

Maybe she needed to accept that as much as she cared for him, as much as she was attracted to him, he wasn't going to be the life partner she wanted.

"I wish I could take Beck from you," Billy said. "It's going to be a hike back up."

"I'm fine with him," she answered. "Honest."

AFTER LEAVING THE national park, Billy suggested they grab lunch and he stopped at historic Ruby's Inn. Lunch was quiet, but not uncomfortably so, and he was content to just focus on his pulled pork sandwich while Erika ate and gave Beck a bottle.

Lunch over, he drove them to Bryce to get shopping done and then midafternoon they were on the way back to his cabin near Hatch.

The drive home was even quieter than lunch. Billy shot Erika a couple of side glances, wondering what she was thinking as she kept her gaze fixed on the landscape beyond her passenger window. From her profile, he couldn't tell if she was upset, but she'd lost her bubbly joy. She was back to being the serious Erika Baylor he'd met in the Wyatt kitchen in Paradise Valley.

He had a nagging sense that she was replaying their earlier conversation over and over in her head. With her psychology training, she could go any number of ways analyzing him, them, the conversation in general. But too much analysis was just as destructive as no analysis. Erika might be book smart, but from what he'd learned of her, she relied too much on books, and placed too much weight on the opinions of so-called experts, when in reality, she should listen to herself. She had a good head on her shoulders. She had strong values, and a solid work ethic. She should trust herself. He trusted her. And he did listen to her. She gave good advice, but she didn't seem inclined to want to take advice from others.

"You okay over there?" he asked.

She nodded.

He wasn't reassured. "What are you thinking about?"

She glanced at him, blue-green eyes somber. "I've been hard on you, and I have no right to be—"

"No harder than my family, and you haven't said things

that Mom or Tommy or Joe haven't said."

"But they're your family. They have a right to weigh in. I don't."

"It's because you care about me," he answered. "I know that."

"I do," she whispered, her eyes filling with tears.

He reached over and briefly put his hand on hers before returning it to the steering wheel since it was the only hand available for steering. "I care about you, too. No need to beat yourself up. Everything's good."

Her shimmering eyes met his. "Is it?"

"Yes." But he wasn't entirely convinced.

They were different people on different paths and at some point they'd go in different directions, and he wasn't looking forward to the day their paths diverged, but until then, he was going to enjoy her, and be her friend, and fight the damn attraction that made him want to get her naked and do all kinds of pleasurable things to her, and with her.

His body reacted to the images in his head, the zipper of his jeans growing tight over the hardening of his body. "Did I ever tell you how I ended up with property in Hatch?" he asked, needing to be distracted.

She wiped her eyes dry and sat up straighter. "No. I've wondered, too, as it seems pretty much off the beaten path."

"It was an impulse purchase. I was upset, a friend was trying to offload some of his property, and I bought it for cash. The transaction took a week and it was done. I owned land in Utah."

"Why were you upset?"

"You'll think I'm crazy."

"That's a given."

He grinned. "You have become very sassy, Miss Baylor, soon to be Dr. Baylor."

"You seem to like it, and I aim to please."

"You can't tell anyone what I'm going to tell you. You must swear to secrecy."

"I can't, if you've committed a murder."

He liked her, she was funny and beautiful, and he enjoyed her quick wit. "No murder, no mayhem, nothing illegal."

"What about immoral?"

"Nope. It's more of a pitiable reaction I had to something someone else did, resulting in me having my own place in the middle of a state where no one in my family lives."

"It had to be something someone in your family did," she said.

"It was. How did you come to that conclusion though?"

"Because they're the only ones that really matter to you, and therefore the only ones that would get under your skin that much."

"Smart girl. If psychology doesn't work out, you could be a detective."

She laughed, the sound bright, tinkly.

"What I'm about to tell you is not known, not by anyone

in my family, and so you must promise to take this secret to your grave."

"I take patient confidentiality very seriously and promise not to disclose what you are about to share with me."

The mock gravity in her voice made him glance at her. She was trying not to smile, and yet her eyes were bright, and her cheeks had picked up color from their hike. Her long golden hair was tousled from the earlier breeze and he thought she looked like heaven, at least his idea of heaven where angels were a bit naughty, and all celestial beings had a sense of humor.

If he had a dream girl, it was Erika. Brilliant, beautiful, warm, kind, funny.

He'd love to love her. She was so sweet and sexy, but he couldn't offer her the stability she craved. He couldn't offer her the love she deserved.

And she deserved all the love in the world.

"I bought the land when Tommy called me to tell me he'd gotten married," he said. "It was a shock. I couldn't wrap my head around it. Tommy was my best friend and he'd married without me there? Without even talking to me about it first? I was in Vegas, too. We were there for the National Finals Rodeo. He and I were sharing a hotel room. How does he go get married without saying a word to me?"

"You were hurt."

"I was angry."

"But hurt," she said.

He sighed. "Hurt, yes. Angry and hurt and I wanted nothing to do with him and his new wife, so I bought the land the next day and moved into the little cabin on the property and that was that. Tommy was no longer my problem."

"Tommy's not married now."

"No."

"How long ago did they divorce?"

"I don't know." Billy glanced her way. "I don't think it lasted long, but he's never discussed it. Any of it."

"What do you mean?"

"What do you mean?"

"We talk about everything, I mean, everything, but he has never shared anything about her, or why he married her, or why they divorced, and I'm the only one in the family who knows about the Vegas wedding."

"Do you even know her name?"

"No. For some reason I kept thinking it was Briar, but I've no proof."

"Briar?"

"I don't even know where I got that from because Tommy doesn't discuss it. He never told anyone else about the wedding, and until now, I never told anyone else. So you're privy to a Wyatt secret."

"Was he drunk when he married her?"

"No."

"Was she pregnant?"

"No idea." Billy glanced at Erika. Her eyes were wide, her expression baffled. "Tommy has never talked about it."

"Why didn't he want the rest of your family to know?"

"Mom made it clear that there were only two things we couldn't fail at—one was marriage and the other was birth control. If we were going to marry, we needed to make it work, and if we were going to have sex, we better condom up."

"And yet you and April…"

"A definite shocker since we'd used protection. I'd used protection."

"So Tommy has kept his secret because he doesn't want to disappoint your mom?"

"No. He's kept his secret because there is more to the story, and for whatever reason, he doesn't want anyone to know the story."

"How long ago was this?"

"Three years? Four? It's been a while now."

"Wow."

"I know." Billy put on the signal for the turn to his property. "And now you've got to keep the secret, too."

She drew her legs up on the seat. "Why did you tell me?"

"Because I trust you." He gave her a long, knowing look. "And I think it's time you trusted yourself."

※

BACK AT THE cabin, Erika showered and dressed, while

playing Billy's words in her head. He trusted her, and he thought it was time she trusted herself.

What did that even mean?

It was so frustrating. He was so frustrating. There was something between them but she had no idea what it was.

He was flirty, and fun, and sometimes serious, but it was never more.

Well, there was that tension, the one they both worked hard to ignore, but sexual tension wasn't a relationship. Sexual tension was what Billy was best at.

He didn't do relationships. He just had sex.

If she was open to it, she thought he'd probably have sex with her.

She wasn't open to it, though. She wanted him, but not that way. Or at least, not only that way. Sex with him wasn't enough. She didn't just want an orgasm, she wanted love. She wanted his heart.

Unlike Billy, she didn't have a close family. She didn't have a clan. She needed people of her own, her family, and she wouldn't settle for less. She couldn't. Love was too important.

Billy grilled steaks that night using just his right arm. He had her help him in the kitchen, washing potatoes and salting before wrapping in foil, and then rinsing the romaine lettuce for a salad. But he seasoned the steaks on his own, and then managed to light and clean the outdoor grill.

She carried the potatoes and platter of steaks outside to

him, and then after checking on Beck, who was bouncing wildly in his bouncy seat, leaned against the column on the back porch and watched Billy put the potatoes on. "We'll need to wait for the steaks," he said.

He'd showered when he returned, and his hair was wet, slicked back, showing off his impressive bone structure. He was a handsome man even straight out of the shower. "Did any of your family wonder about you buying a cabin in southwest Utah?"

"Joe was disappointed. He's hoping some of us will settle on the ranch, help him out, but that's not me. Who knows? Tommy might."

"Don't you miss your mom and grandfather when you're here?"

"I try to see them every month or two, even if just for a day. Planning on taking Beck home before too long. Thinking of heading there for Mother's Day."

"When is Mother's Day?" she asked.

"Mid May, second Sunday of May, I believe." His eyebrows lifted. "I thought all women knew stuff like that."

"The last time I sent my mom a card it came back unopened." She shrugged. "I never bothered to send another one. If she doesn't want a relationship with me, I'm not going to force it."

"But you miss her."

"I miss..." She exhaled and the words died. It didn't matter. It wasn't going to change her mom, or her family dynamics. You couldn't make people want you. You couldn't make people love you. They either did, or they didn't. Better to come to terms with reality, better to have acceptance. "Actually, I don't miss her. I don't miss the family I was raised with. It wasn't ideal."

"You fight with yourself all the time."

"What do you mean?"

"I think you want acceptance, but don't have it. And I think you want a family, but you're not sure you'll get it… or you deserve it. Which I think is crazy because you're one of the most together women I've ever met—"

"Not saying a lot, based on the women you meet."

"Do you have a boyfriend?"

"No."

"Why not?"

"I'm too invested in my degree."

"Just because you're studying, doesn't mean you can't date, or have someone serious in your life."

"Maybe I haven't met anyone that I liked enough to include in my life."

"That's fair," he replied.

There was something about the conversation that made her breath catch, and her heart ache. He made her feel so much. She didn't know how he did it.

Erika turned away and gazed out, focusing on the horizon. The sun was beginning to set, long golden rays of light outlining the hills, dappling the field below the cabin with shadows. A deer grazed in the shadowed pasture, and then a fawn, carefully picking its way through the grass to join its mother.

"Do you see?" Billy asked, pointing to the pasture.

She nodded. "Love it. You're lucky to have a little slice of paradise. No traffic, no noise, no neighbors. Just deer."

"And coyotes, raccoons, skunks, birds." He opened the lid on the grill and turned the potatoes over before adding the steaks. "I've never been here for this long at one time. It's been good." He closed the lid. "The steaks won't take long. Want to check on Beck? Maybe finish up the salad? I'll be inside in just a bit."

Erika returned to the kitchen, made the salad and lifted Beck from his bouncy seat, carrying him on her hip as she lifted down the dishes, and brought the butter and sour cream from the refrigerator. She could hear Billy's voice from outside. Glancing out the French doors, she could see he was on the phone talking to someone.

She couldn't hear very much, just a few words here and there. Trip. Mother's Day. And then something about a rodeo.

Erika strained to hear more, but Billy wasn't saying much, just answering with one-word replies now and then.

She looked down at Beck who was doing his best to worm his hand into her mouth and she kissed it instead. "Everything is good," she said to him. "Everything is great."

Chapter Ten

THE NEXT MORNING, Erika struggled to get real work done. She'd been sitting on her bed for a couple hours but was stuck on the same sentence.

Frustrated, she climbed off the bed and headed for the kitchen to refresh her water glass. The living room was empty. No Beck and no Billy.

On her way back to her room she checked the two other bedrooms. They were both empty as well. Where were the boys? What were they doing?

She left the house, her gaze sweeping the corral, seeing just the horses outside grazing. As she entered the barn she could hear Billy's voice.

"You're not going to start roping from the saddle. That's not how we're going to do it. We'll just start with a rope just like this, and the dummy head. We're going to do lots and lots of drills, building muscle memory, so your body remembers what it's doing, no matter what the horse does."

She peeked around the stable to an open area of the barn where Billy had spread a blanket on the ground and propped Beck up against a saddle. Billy was practicing roping the dummy head positioned on a hay bale. "Nice and easy," he said, throwing the rope and catching the dummy's horns perfectly. "Always both horns. You need the tip of the rope to go over the horns smoothly. It's going to take a lot of practice, but you'll get it. I used to do this a hundred times a day or more when I was a boy. You'll need to wear a glove or you'll tear up your hand, but even then you're going to get calluses. You want calluses. Otherwise your hands will always be a mess."

"Getting him ready for the rodeo circuit?" she said, stepping around the door, and into view.

"He's a Wyatt. He's going to need to know how to rope."

She didn't contradict him, she simply smiled and returned to the house, and her room, and the computer.

She felt angry, though, as she closed the door of the bedroom and then sat back down on her bed with the computer.

She didn't want to be in here, not while they were out there. She wanted to be with them. She liked being with them, and in their company, she relaxed, something she'd always found it hard to do. The more time she spent here at the cabin, the more relaxed she felt. She'd never been someone who just hung out. She was always doing something, reading something, trying to accomplish more things, but in the past few weeks she'd wanted to read less and accomplish less, and just… be.

Just breathe.

She picked up her laptop but her heart wasn't in it. She thought of all the things she'd rather be doing.

Going for a drive.

Doing another hike.

Stopping somewhere for lunch and homemade pie.

She wanted more of the life she'd experienced lately, more companionship, more fun, more happiness. The life she wanted was here, but it wasn't hers, not forever. If only it could be. If only the dream could be a reality.

˜

THE WEEK PASSED slowly, with Erika more anxious by the day about her dissertation. She wasn't getting it done. She wasn't making sufficient progress. The guilt and worry filled her. She was in trouble, but she struggled with the isolation in her room.

While she battled, Billy was healing, becoming more mobile by the day. He'd stopped wearing his sling as consistently as he had in the beginning. She tried to caution him against doing too much but she noticed he ignored her feedback and did what he wanted.

He was trying hard to keep Beck busy, too, taking him from her for big chunks of the day so she could work, and Erika appreciated it, but since she wasn't making significant progress, she just felt bad that Billy was trying so hard to help her and she couldn't even help herself.

Today was one of the worst days in a long time, too. Erika couldn't even focus enough to write a sentence. A sentence! She'd draft one sentence, then delete it. Then rewrite it. Then delete it.

Erika felt like hurling her computer across the room. This wasn't working. *She* wasn't working. Was it bad to just want to enjoy herself?

Erika had never cared much for TV—she didn't even own one at the moment—but in the past couple of weeks her favorite thing to do was watch the nightly news with Billy, and then every evening after Beck was put to bed, they'd watch a program, and talk. They talked about everything and even though they frequently had different viewpoints, Billy always listened to her thoughts, just as she listened to his. She even liked his TV programs which were different from anything she'd ever watched—*Gold Rush* and *Building Off the Grid*.

He liked DIY programs and learning how to build things and just last night she asked if he'd ever built anything and he'd nodded, gesturing to the space they were in. "This," he'd said.

"This cabin?" she'd asked.

"I hired a builder, but I worked alongside him. Every moment when I wasn't competing, I was here."

"It must have saved you a lot of money."

"It would have, if I'd stopped upgrading everything." He smiled. "But I enjoyed being part of the build. It was really satisfying."

"And the barn? Same builder?"

"No. I did that, with Tommy, after the house was completed. You'll notice it's pretty basic in comparison."

But the barn wasn't basic, and Billy's skills weren't basic, but he was so modest, never wanting compliments, uncomfortable being fussed over. Was it being the third son that had made him uncomfortable being praised, or was he not praised very often growing up?

He'd told her he'd been dyslexic, he'd said he'd struggled in school, he'd clearly resented being made to feel as if he wasn't bright enough. Good enough. It stirred her sympathy because he was just the opposite—bright, hardworking, nonjudgmental of others.

A truly good person.

Last night, as they finished watching the TV show, she'd snuck glances at him, taking in the big shoulders, his broad chest, and that beautiful face of his. Just looking at him made her insides feel fluttery. So fluttery.

She was head over heels. Nothing good could come of this. But it was too late to turn back, too late to save herself. She was already in way too deep.

※

AFTER DINNER THAT evening, Billy watched Erika give Beck a bath in the kitchen sink. The sleeves on her red sweater were pushed up to her elbows, her long blonde hair high in a ponytail on the top of her head. She had bubbles on one forearm, and a small cluster of bubbles on her chin. She was happy, laughing, as Beck vigorously splashed bath water. The more she laughed, the harder Beck splashed, sending water and suds everywhere.

She looked like she could be Beck's mom. They were both fair, they both had light eyes, they both laughed with the same joy.

Beck seemed to think she was his mom. He lit up every time she entered the room. And thanks to Erika's attention, Beck was becoming a very contented baby. He gurgled and cooed, and made babbling noises as he waved his hands.

But then, how could anyone be unhappy around Erika? Lately, she was full of sunshine and light, confidence and optimism.

He felt protective of her. He loved it when she laughed, loved making her laugh, and he tried to make her laugh as much as he could.

He rose from his chair and stepped into the kitchen. "I'm thinking of going home for Mother's Day. Do you want to go with us?"

She reached for a washcloth and wiped bubbles from her eyelashes. "Is that a good idea?" she asked.

"Why wouldn't it be?"

"Just don't want to give your family the wrong idea about us."

He frowned. "What do you mean?"

"I just think if I show up with you, they're going to think

it's odd that I'm still hanging around two months later."

"They know you're here. They know you're the one taking care of Beck since I was hurt."

"Yes, but it's one thing for me to be here, and another in your family's home. I don't want your mom or granddad to think we have a relationship when we don't. It doesn't seem fair to give them ideas."

"That won't happen. They know me."

Her expression flickered, her smile slipping before she managed to save it. "Well, that's a relief." She turned away from him and pushed up her sleeves higher on her elbows before picking up a towel and reaching for Beck. "Okay, Stormtrooper, we're getting out."

Was it his imagination or had she dismissed him? "Need a hand?" Billy asked.

She didn't even look at him. "Nope. I've got it. Go back to your show. I'm good here."

And she was good, he thought. She was more than good, and she'd carried more than her fair share of the weight around here. She'd managed Beck, managed the house, had even managed him.

Now she was managing to do without him.

He didn't like it.

He liked doing things together, being together, being partners with her. He wasn't a fan of being told to go, leave. He didn't like feeling shut out in his own house.

She was angry with him, and it had to do with his visit to

Paradise Valley, as well as other things, things they didn't discuss. Like the tension simmering between them, a sexual tension he'd never felt with anyone else.

They'd spent weeks together in this cabin without a kiss, weeks where they'd tripped over each other, and avoided each other, weeks where the chemistry crackled and burned.

Billy was done tiptoeing around the attraction, pretending it didn't exist. He was done tiptoeing around Erika, not wanting to offend her with his constant desire. He wouldn't apologize for being attracted to her, and he wouldn't apologize for wanting her.

Because he did want her, he dreamed of taking her to his bed, night after night. He wanted to touch her and feel her. Wanted her mouth and her tongue and her body, every bit he could have, every bit he could touch and taste.

After putting Beck to bed, she returned to the kitchen to rinse out the sink and put the baby shampoo and bath toys away. He'd already done it, though, and when she looked down into the empty, clean sink she then turned toward him, surprised. "Thank you," she said. "That was nice of you."

He'd left his chair and was standing on the far side of the kitchen island. "Nice that I'd take care of my son?"

Her chin lifted, and he didn't know if she was responding to his words or tone. "I only meant that it was nice to have your help. I appreciate it."

"I try to help."

"I have never said you don't." Her gaze met his, expression fierce. "You're picking a fight."

"You started it."

"I did?" She laughed, even as her hands went to her hips, drawing his eye to her waist, her breasts, her legs. "I don't think so. I wasn't the one who suggested dragging me to Montana as if I was the nanny."

"That's not how I invited you."

"But it's the role I play. Beck's caregiver. Beck's cousin. Beck's special buddy."

"You're being ridiculous."

"Maybe," she agreed. "Or maybe I've just had it with being convenient. Maybe I'm tired of being that cheerful, giving woman who is here to make your life easier—"

"You're not that cheerful," he interrupted. "And you're far from convenient." He marched to her, closing the distance between them. "In fact, what I feel for you is incredibly inconvenient."

She blinked up at him, lips parting slightly. "You have feelings for me?"

"Hunger. Need. Want. Desire that never goes away."

Two bright spots of color flamed in her cheeks. "I suppose I should be flattered."

"You've lived in this house with me for weeks and it's all I can do to keep my distance. I'm tired of keeping my distance. Tired of pretending you're not beautiful, not tempting, not driving me crazy." He caught her by the wrist and drew her toward him, pulling her against him, even as he shifted his left arm away, keeping it from being jostled. "I want you, Erika. I want you bad."

Her head tipped back, and her bright glowing eyes met his. "You only want me because you can't have me."

"Not true. I want you because you're the most beautiful woman I've ever met and you fill my thoughts and you haunt my dreams, and I wake up every morning aching for you." His head dropped, his lips brushing the curve of her warm cheek. She smelled like coconut cream, reminding him of summer and sunny beaches and icy blended cocktails. "At the same time, I'm not going to force you into kissing me. I don't want to do anything you don't want. So if you want me to let you go, tell me now, and I will. I'll let you go and I'll walk out of here and we'll act like this has never happened."

"Even though it happened?"

He laughed, a rumble of mocking sound. "*Nothing* has happened, and nothing will happen if you're not interested."

He felt the tremor course through her, her slim frame swaying, her breasts brushing his chest even as her gaze searched his, the tip of her tongue darting out to touch her upper lip. "You know I like you," she said lowly, as if in protest.

"Not half as much as I like you."

Heat flared in her eyes, and she swayed against him again. He slid his right arm around her, his palm on the small of her back, pressing her closer. She shuddered at the contact, leaning against him more fully, and his body went hot and hard. She was warm, soft, everything he liked and he dropped his head, and captured her mouth with his.

She tasted like cinnamon and sugar and he had to have more. He parted her lips, tongue stroking her soft mouth, and then inside of her mouth, showing her just what he wanted to do to her body. Love it. Taste it. Devour it.

She whimpered and pressed closer. He stroked up her back, his hand sliding under her hair to her soft nape, his palm cupping the back of her head, fingers pressing against her scalp. The kiss was hot and hungry, full of weeks of pent-up desire. She looked like an angel but kissed like sin and he didn't think he'd ever get enough of her.

Erika stood on tiptoe and wrapped her arms around his neck. He walked her backward until he'd pushed her against the counter, the better to lean into her body, the better for creating pressure and friction.

She must have liked the pressure of his erection against his thighs because she whimpered and shifted her hips, trying to capture more sensation. The sexy shift of her hips made him harden further. If she wanted pleasure, he knew just how to deliver. He'd make her feel so good she'd never want anyone else, ever again.

The very idea of her with anyone else made him feel possessive, and he never felt possessive. How could he when he didn't want a relationship?

But kissing Erika, touching her, made him think that just maybe there was no one else he wanted to touch, and kiss, but her.

And the realization that he wanted to be the one for her, the only one, shocked him. He broke off the kiss, stared down into her lovely eyes, eyes cloudy with passion and the sweet heat of their kiss, and wondered what had just happened? She'd just rocked his world but he didn't know what to do about it.

Didn't know what to do with her.

Normally, he'd take a woman to bed at this point, but there was no taking Erika to bed. That wasn't the logical next step. Problem was, there was no logical next step. Not with her. Not now. Maybe not ever.

※

IN HER BEDROOM, Erika sank onto the edge of her bed, fingertips pressed to her swollen lips.

That kiss was so good.

So unbelievably hot.

She exhaled slowly, lips still tingling, pulse thudding. She felt boneless. Spineless. Her insides hot, molten… matching the need aching within her.

She wanted him, wanted so much more of him, and it didn't make sense because she knew him and he wasn't what she needed, but oh, she wanted him. She'd never felt this way before. She literally felt as if she burned… that he'd lit a fire inside of her and the fire had to be answered. The fire needed more heat, more touch, more of him.

She knew who he was, too. She knew all too well how he operated. But her body didn't care, and her heart, well, that had never listened very well to her, either.

Her heart had a mind of its own and for some reason it just thought Billy Wyatt was it. The beginning and the end and everything in between.

※

ERIKA WASN'T THE only one rattled by the kiss. Billy was in trouble. He already felt so much respect for her. Respect, and admiration, and trust. The chemistry had been there, too, chemistry that had drawn him in from the start, but he hadn't expected a kiss to confuse him.

Kisses weren't confusing.

But that one was.

After walking away from her in the kitchen, he'd headed outside. The sun had come and gone, the sky was lavender in places, and purple in others. He walked to the corral, empty now, his horses in their stalls in the barn for the night, and leaned into the top railing. He felt turned inside out, his chest all knotted, his gut cramping with needles and pins.

Erika.

Man, she'd felt good. Unbelievably good. As he'd stroked the length of her, she'd shivered and arched and her sensitivity had driven him wild. If just kissing her fully clothed was that electric, he couldn't imagine her in bed. Or, he could, and it made him hard, and throb, as if he were an inexperienced kid. But he wasn't inexperienced, and he'd had more than his fair share of women, but he couldn't remember any woman turning him on this much.

He couldn't remember feeling so primal about a woman, either.

When she'd been in his arms, all he could think was mine. Mine, mine, mine.

Crazy.

He wasn't possessive, he didn't ever feel a need to lay claim to a woman. Why would he, when he didn't think long-term? But tonight, kissing Erika, he did. He wanted her, and it had crossed his mind that if he were a caveman, he'd throw her over his shoulder and run to his cave, make love to her there so that she'd never leave his bearskin. Never leave his fire.

The fact that he was even thinking these thoughts meant he'd lost his mind.

He'd spent too much time in the cabin, too much time in lockdown. He needed to get back on the road, back to his world of asphalt and trailers, parking lots and competition. A couple weeks of tough rides and hard falls should clear his head and remind him who he was.

A confirmed bachelor.

A man without commitments.

Because he didn't commit. He didn't fall in love. He

couldn't promise her forever.

Until he was traveling again, he had to be careful to put distance between them.

Actual, physical distance, as well as more boundaries—space, time apart, less intimate situations. And certainly, no more touching, no more kissing, no more displays of affection.

❦

THE NEXT MORNING, after coffee, Billy exiled himself to the barn. He didn't want eggs. He just wanted to be alone. It was the first time he'd spent an entire morning outside since his injury, and even though there were things he couldn't do, there was a lot he could. He focused on the horses, and mucking stalls one-handed, and then gingerly bridling and saddling each, exercising both in the corral attached to the barn. It felt good to be in the saddle again, and even though his goal had been to exercise them, he realized he had needed the exercise, too.

Erika appeared twice that morning, long blonde hair in a loose side braid, offering fresh coffee, and then later, wondering if he wanted lunch. He declined both offers and made a light remark about how he'd been sitting too much and eating too much and it was time to get back in shape.

She looked worried but bit back whatever it was she wanted to say. He watched her return to the house, his gut tight, the air bottled in his chest because she could tell things were different between them and was worried she'd done something. He wanted to reassure her that she hadn't done anything other than kiss him far too well, but how did you even have that conversation? You didn't. So, as the cabin door closed behind her, he forced his attention back to his ride, nudging his gelding into a sprint across the soft dirt.

※

IT WAS OBVIOUS Billy was avoiding her, and Erika gave him space all day, but by dinner time she'd had enough of his cagey distance and silence. She'd made a roast chicken, something that wasn't hard, not after she looked up recipes online and was proud of her efforts, but then angry when Billy barely ate.

"No breakfast," she said, sitting back at the table, "no lunch and now hardly any dinner. What's going on? Are you sick? In pain? Do I need to get you to a doctor?"

"Nothing's wrong," he retorted, pushing aside his plate. "Just not hungry. Don't take it personally."

"You're always hungry, so yes, I'm taking it personally."

"Well, don't. Everything's fine—"

"No, it's not." She reached for Beck's plastic key ring and handed it back to him. "Things are not fine. You've shut me out, given me the big freeze, and, after last night, it's kind of hurt my feelings." Erika gave him a long, assessing look. "Was the kiss that disappointing? Did I not respond appropriately?"

He winced. "It wasn't bad, and you know it."

"No, I don't know it. All I know is that you pushed me away from you last night and haven't spoken more than a half dozen words since." She swallowed hard but kept her composure. "Can you just fill me in so I know what's going on here?"

"Do you really not know?"

"No. And I'm not in the mood for guessing games. Just treat me like I have half a brain and tell me what's going on."

Billy stared at her a long minute. "I'm attracted to you."

"Okay."

"It's not okay. It's a problem."

"Why?"

"Because I'm not going to muck our friendship up by making another move on you."

"Because I'm April's cousin?"

"No. Because you're you. You're not looking for a good time. You're looking for a forever man, and that's not me. We both know that. Don't we?"

She swallowed and gave a short nod, even as a part of her silently argued with him. He wasn't as shallow as he claimed. He wasn't the player he pretended to be. But at the same time, if he didn't want more with her, he didn't want more.

"Okay then," she said, rising from the table. "I'll wash up."

Chapter Eleven

For the next few weeks Billy and Erika maintained a polite façade of somewhat icy cordiality. She still made him breakfast in the morning, and they still watched TV in the evening, but there was little conversation. They'd watch the news and programs in silence and then Erika would excuse herself and go to bed.

May first came and went, and Erika paid rent yet again on an apartment she hadn't seen since February.

Every day, she disappeared into her room after breakfast while Billy took care of Beck so she could work.

Her progress was laughable, though. If she were being honest, it had ground to a stop. Like today, she just sat with her computer, and stared across the room, anxious, worried, heartsick.

She was in trouble in so many ways. She wasn't working, wasn't being practical, wasn't being realistic. She'd unplugged too much from her own life and was too caught up in what was happening here in this corner of southwest Utah.

She loved the cabin, and the isolation. She loved Beck,

and Billy. She loved the fantasy she'd helped create—being here was like playing house. She could almost pretend she was the mom, Billy was the dad, Beck was their baby. She could almost pretend that she and Billy had a relationship. She could almost pretend that things would work out and they'd be together, a happy ever after.

But she knew.

She knew the truth. She was just avoiding it and reality.

Sighing, Erika forced her attention back to her computer screen, and lifted her hands, fingertips hovering over the keyboard. She reread her last paragraph, but no thoughts came, nothing she could write down. Fighting tears, Erika flipped through her notes, waiting for inspiration, or just for her brain to engage. She had to pull it together. She needed to focus. She couldn't sit here daydreaming, wasting time in wishful thinking. She had work to do, and it was time she got it done—

Her vision blurred, tears blinding her.

She reached up and wiped them away, filled with self-loathing. When had she become so pathetic? What was wrong with her? This was her work, her job, her *life*.

But was it?

Did it have to be?

Was it so wrong to want a break, to want to focus on the here and now?

Erika stared at her computer screen for a long moment, then glanced out the window, toward the distant pink mountains. Every day, she thought of the drive and the hike. She remembered the sheer joy of being outside, moving, living, breathing. The joy of being in the moment. The joy of just feeling good, of feeling needed.

That was what she wanted. That was all she wanted right now.

Decision made, Erika opened her email and composed a message to her department chair, as well as her own advisor. She wasn't giving up, but she was stepping away, at least for a little while.

❧

ERIKA WASN'T SURE how to tell Billy about her decision, or the email she'd sent to her academic advisor. He wouldn't like it, and she worried he might blame himself, but she hadn't done it for him. She'd done it for herself.

At the same time, Billy was healing remarkably well. He'd gone to Cedar City twice to be seen by doctors, and on the last visit, he'd had an appointment with a physical therapist who'd sent him home with stretches and gentle exercises. But Billy didn't do anything gently, and within days was back to working out, and the active life he'd led.

Boom still came over to assist with certain chores, but Erika suspected Billy just liked Boom's company, and wanted to shoot the breeze with him. Billy seemed most comfortable outside, or in the barn.

She said as much one day, early in May. "You're recovering fast. Even faster than the doctors expected."

"It's good. I don't like feeling helpless. I hated adding to your worries when you've had so much pressure on you with your dissertation."

This was probably the time to tell him she wasn't feeling pressure, not anymore, and wouldn't feel pressure for quite some time since she'd asked for an extension and had been granted it.

But she didn't say it, because her mind was on other things, like Billy, and that kiss from a few weeks ago, and how she wished every day he'd kiss her again. How she wished right now he'd kiss her again. He was standing so close, smelling of hay and sunshine, looking even more gorgeous, if such a thing was possible. Faint creases fanned at his eyes, and there was a little groove next to his mouth that deepened when he smiled. She'd come to know his face so well, and it was a face she loved to study when he wasn't paying attention to her.

"It was never a hardship," she said, fingers itching to reach out and grab his belt, and pull him toward her. She'd loved those weeks where he'd needed her help with bandages and slings. It had been too long since he'd needed her help and she could feel his warmth, and the press of that impressive chest. "You never complained, and you always did try to help me, despite your limitations."

Suddenly he reached out and brushed a long tendril of her hair back, tucking it behind her ear. "You've gotten pretty good at eggs. Scrambled and fried. I'm impressed."

She pursed her lips, trying not to smile. He was so lovely and awful at the same time. She never knew if she wanted to punch him or kiss him—

Okay, not true.

She was desperate to kiss him again. Her body hummed with tension all day long, her skin so sensitive, lips tingling. If only he'd kiss her and maybe it wouldn't be as good as the first time. Maybe she'd realize that had been a fluke, and she'd not want his mouth on hers, or kissing his way down her neck, or covering her nipple—

"Nipple?" he said. "What?"

Erika threw her head back, horrified, her gaze locking with his. "What did you say?"

"What did you say? Nipple?"

Heat burned her cheeks, her face blisteringly hot. "*No.* Why would I say that?"

"I don't know." His gaze dropped and lingered on her breasts. "But now that you mention it—"

"I didn't mention it. You did. I don't even know what's going on." Flustered, she marched to the sink, checking for dirty dishes. There were none. She looked at the coffeepot. It was empty. Maybe she should make a fresh pot. "Do you want some coffee?" she asked, tone brisk.

He laughed softly behind her. "No."

"Lunch?"

"Had lunch already."

"Snack?"

He didn't answer, and the silence wasn't quiet, but a taut, listening awareness that made her insides do a funny flip, and the hair rise on her nape. Even without looking at him, she knew he was looking at her, and she could feel the heat in his eyes, feel the sizzling energy between them. It had been like this for weeks now. No physical contact, just endless sparks and tingling awareness, an awareness that made her chest tight and her body ache.

She glanced at him over her shoulder and her gaze met his, his intense blue gaze smoldering, filled with unspoken desire. "No Cheez-Its?" she murmured, hot and shivery at the same time.

"No."

His voice was deep and hard, his jaw equally hard, his mouth firm, uncompromising. She couldn't even imagine being his woman. Couldn't imagine the heat or passion. She'd had sex before, but it wasn't with anyone like Billy. But honestly, was there anyone like Billy? Tough, competitive, smart, grounded, funny—so funny.

She'd never been so attracted to anyone physically before, not like this. Billy made her want and need. He made her want everything and that was so new, and so shocking, she still hadn't been able to wrap her head around it. The desire. The desire for him.

But the desire came with emotions, and unlike simple lust, she didn't want to just sleep with him. She wanted the whole package... all of him. His heart along with his body, but he didn't do relationships. He didn't invest in women for the long haul. If they went to bed together, that was all it would be—sex. A carnal itch that might be briefly satisfied but would ultimately leave her feeling worse. Feeling emptier, more alone.

More broken.

She couldn't handle that.

What she needed was someone who'd want her for love, but also life. Someone who'd want to be with her when she wasn't young and she didn't have a small waist and firm butt. She wanted someone who'd love her with wrinkles and gray hair. Someone who'd make her laugh just because he enjoyed making her laugh.

"Goldfish?" she said, eyes hot and stinging. Heart filling her throat.

"Do we have any?" he asked.

"No."

The corner of his mouth lifted, and his eyes burned into hers. "Good try."

"Thank you."

"I think you know what I want," he said after a moment.

She did, too. She wanted the same thing. As his gaze held hers, she could feel the leashed desire, the hunger contained. She knew he wanted her. His energy was potent. Powerful. His interest made her feel almost beautiful, and that was something as she'd never felt beautiful, not even when people paid her compliments. It was hard to feel beautiful when you knew you were deeply flawed, when you weren't sure you were whole enough to be truly loved. She'd grown up all too aware of her fears and foibles; the insecurities that made her feel shame.

But somehow, when she was with Billy, close to him, she didn't feel shame. She didn't feel broken. She felt alive and fierce. Hopeful. But all it would take was one misstep and then the beautiful desire, and the lovely sense of wanting, and being wanted, would end.

"I don't want to be one of your girls," she said, grateful she could sound calm, relaxed, when she felt anything but.

"This is getting harder, not easier," he said abruptly.

She nodded.

"What are we going to do about it?" he asked.

She could see from his eyes what he wanted to do. Her pulse thudded, her heart felt as if it had tumbled to her feet. "What do you want to do?"

"Maybe I should get on the road again. Join Tommy—"

"You're going to compete?"

"Just travel with him. Keep him company."

Her eyes smarted. "And leave Beck here with me?"

"Boom's mom has offered to babysit regularly—"

"So, you do mean to leave us behind."

"I know you have work to do, and it's hard being locked down here. I've nothing to do. I'm just in your way."

Something in his tone made her chest tighten. He was

creating boundaries. Distancing himself. Pushing her away again. "This your home. Maybe it's time for me to go. You're six weeks post-surgery. You can do almost everything—"

"Beck will miss you."

Beck. But not Billy, not him. It was hard to swallow around the lump blocking her throat. "I love Beck. It will be hard to leave him, but I know he's in good hands with you."

He didn't immediately reply. "No one is telling you to leave."

"Thank goodness. That would be mortifying." She struggled to smile, and held it there, as if it'd been slapped onto her face. "But I'll always be in his life. If you let me."

"Of course I'll let you. You're his family."

His family, meaning Beck's family. Never, ever Billy's. The distinction was so clear, and so painful, but it was what she needed to hear. Billy wouldn't love her. He'd never willingly choose her. "There's something I should tell you. It will probably be a relief, but I've asked for, and have received, an extension on my dissertation."

"You won't be graduating when you planned?"

"I couldn't get motivated, couldn't get anything done. I'd just sit at my computer and stare at the screen and it made me feel worse about things, and life's too short for that."

"You should have told me. I would have gotten help. I could have reached out to Ellen and asked if she'd be interested in coming over every day—"

"I'm happy to have a break. I need it. Ever since February, I've been tied up in knots, feeling torn, feeling guilty, and I'm over it. I just want to feel good for a bit, I just want to feel okay."

"You were almost done, Erika. You were so close."

"Not close enough. And I'm not walking away forever, just pushing away from the desk for now."

"It feels like you're quitting. Quitting is never okay."

"Says he that wants to get back on a bucking bull and break what's left of his body."

He ignored the jab. "I feel like I let you down. I'd promised you'd be able to work—"

"And you did give me time to work. I was the one who didn't want to be alone in the bedroom. I wanted to be with you and Beck."

Billy looked at her a long moment, his disappointment evident. "You weren't missing anything, sweetheart. Beck and I would have been here when you're done."

"But that's not true. Once you're strong enough, you'll be back on the rodeo circuit, back to Mr. VIP, everybody's favorite cowboy."

"I'm no one's favorite cowboy."

Her eyes smarted. She struggled to smile. "Not so," she said huskily. "You're mine."

He looked at her a long time before kissing her forehead, and walking out the door without a word.

DINNER WAS ALMOST normal that night. Beck had just started on his first food—baby cereal, and they'd taken turns trying to feed him, laughing at the enthusiasm he applied to the bites. Beck loved food, just like his dad, Erika teased.

Billy had wrinkled his nose. "Not that food," he answered. "Steak, potatoes."

"Eggs," she chimed in.

"Eggs," he agreed.

After dinner, Billy had cleaned Beck up and had gone to put him to bed. Erika was doing the last of the dishes. It had been a nice evening, surprisingly fun. Things had been so serious between them for the past few weeks it was good to hear Billy laugh, to see his smiles. He had the best smile.

Erika turned off the faucet, listening to the pinging noise coming from the living room. It was Billy's phone. He was getting texts, one after the other. She stood at the sink trying to ignore it, but at the same time, unable to focus on anything else. Who would be blowing up his phone on a Saturday evening? He didn't normally get a lot of texts, at least not that she'd heard, and it crossed her mind it could be one of his brothers, and then she worried that maybe something serious had happened. Maybe something to his mom, or grandfather?

Drying her hands, she crossed to the living room and the side table next to his chair and glanced down at Billy's phone. It was face up, revealing new messages. She could only see part of them but the texts were from two different women, Carrie, and a Michelle. It was the one from Carrie that kept pinging, the latest text reading, *"OMG! So bleeping excited to see you for the Fourth!!!"* And then while she stood there, another new one arrived. *"I wasn't sure you'd be riding after your accident but happy I'm going to see you."* Followed by a bunch of emojis Erika didn't want to see.

Erika put the phone back down and returned to the kitchen. She reached for the skillet, intending to wash it next, but once her hands were submerged in hot water, she couldn't do anything.

He was going to be competing again. He was planning on returning to the circuit by the Fourth. Meaning, the Fourth of July?

Her hands shook as she scrubbed the skillet and then rinsed it and set it on the counter. She was trying to stay calm but her temper flared. She didn't know what upset her more. Saturday night texts from a Carrie and Michelle, or discovering that Billy planned to be competing again soon. The Fourth of July was less than two months away. And that was crazy. He couldn't even use his left arm completely. How could he ride, rope, or worse, risk more injury? It was beyond stupid. It was insane. And she was livid.

She'd known he would, but in her mind it had been in the fall, or maybe even next year. Not in a mere matter of weeks. How could he possibly think he could go back out there when he wasn't 100 percent? And why did Carrie know this and not her?

Why was he even texting with Carrie right now? And Michelle? And God knew who else?

Erika was so angry she couldn't even think straight. She gave up trying to dry the remaining dishes and stood in the kitchen, staring out the window over the sink, seeing the sliver of moon in the sky, feeling cheated. Betrayed.

And yet, had he ever promised her more?

They had no relationship. They had no bond. Just because they'd kissed didn't mean there was anything serious between them.

But still, it made her feel sick that she was fantasizing about a life with him while he was texting other women letting them know he couldn't wait to be back on the road so he could see them.

She swore under her breath, curse words she never used, even as she blinked back hot stinging tears, tears of shame and rage. How naïve had she been? How stupid was she?

Her gaze fell on the highchair that needed wiping down, and she sniffled, holding back tears. What about Beck? How could Billy put himself in danger again so soon? It was selfish. Reckless. Beck deserved better. Beck deserved a father who was planning on sticking around, whole, intact, healthy. A father that would be available for Beck's needs, not in hospitals, not in bed, not in casts or slings, not with a walker or wheelchair. Billy was the only one who could decide to be that father. He was the only one who could choose to do the right thing. And the right thing was for him to get well, stay well, and take care of his son.

Billy emerged just then from Beck's bedroom, wearing just a pair of gray flannel pajama pants. He was holding his shirt in his hand. She could see the scars from his recent surgery, the dark pink skin where he'd been patched back together, skin still tender and healing. He walked toward her with the shirt dangling from his hand. "I think I played a little too hard with him. He spewed some of his milk on me."

She just looked at him. Her expression must have told him she wasn't happy because he stopped, gave her a long, wary look.

"What's wrong?" he asked.

"What's wrong? Maybe the fact that you're planning on competing in less than six weeks. Maybe the fact that you're planning on being up in Calgary for some stampede—"

"How did you find out?"

"Is it true then?"

"That's neither here nor there. Who told you?"

Erika's hands squeezed into fists. She pressed them against her rib cage. "Your phone kept buzzing and buzzing and I was worried something had happened to someone in your family." Her voice faded, her shoulder shifting. "But it was only your girlfriends checking in, excited to be with you again. I shouldn't be surprised. I knew who you were from the beginning—"

"What does that mean?"

"I think you know. You made it really clear in the beginning. You don't stick around. Women are just for fun. You have a hookup in every town."

"I never said that."

"You didn't have to. It was pretty easy to figure out. April, the blonde from Las Vegas. The brunette in Tucson. The redhead in San Antonio."

He widened his stance, feet planted shoulder width apart. "I don't really see how my private life is any of your business."

Those were the wrong words. Absolutely the wrong thing for him to say. None of her business? What had she been doing here all spring?

Fresh rage rolled through her, rage and indignation. "Obviously, I don't matter here. I'm just one more female to make your life comfortable. I could be anyone. You could replace me like that." She snapped her fingers. "I could be hired help, someone you booked from a domestic agency. All you have to do is contact one of those sitting services and I'd be replaced."

"I never asked you to give up your whole life for me. I never asked you to sacrifice everything. You volunteered. You said let me stay until you're on your feet again. You said you wanted to be the one with Beck, you said—"

"I know perfectly well what I said, but I had no idea that while I struggled to help you and Beck you were sending sexy texts to women, letting them know when you'd be back in town. The good time cowboy—"

"Is that what you really think of me?"

"Don't act injured. This is your persona. It's who you want to be, who you want everyone to see. Hit Billy Wyatt up for a good time."

"You're not stuck here, Erika. Not trapped. If you're so miserable, go. We don't need you playing Nurse Nightingale. We can manage without you."

Again, the wrong words for him to say. His words felt like gasoline hitting a fire. She just exploded, something she never, ever did. "Wow, glad we got that squared away. Thanks for explaining a lot of things I was clueless about."

She left the kitchen and returned to her room, carefully closing the door behind her, not wanting to wake Beck.

For a long minute, she just stood, back pressed to the door, hands pinned beneath her backside, trying to stop them from trembling. She was in over her head. Go, stay, it was all the same. No matter what she did now, it would crush her. Badly.

Despite her best intentions, she'd become one of those women who held out hope that a man could change, or would change. She'd held out hope that Billy would fall in love with her, and want a life together, that those walls he'd put up around his heart would tumble down, and he'd realize that she was his other half, the one he'd been waiting for.

And yet how many times had he told her he didn't love? That he was the Wyatt who didn't fall in love? She'd known all of this from day one, and yet she'd still secretly hoped.

Prayed.

Believed.

She could see why she'd hoped and believed. It was easy being with Billy, so easy spending time with him. He was smart and sexy and incredibly loving with Beck. He was funny, kind, interesting. Just watching TV with him was entertaining. Going for a drive to Bryce had been the highlight of her stay. Lunch at that historic inn diner had been a treat. They'd wandered through the gift shop, showing each other this and that, as if they were a couple.

There were so many times they felt like a couple, where he, Billy Wyatt, felt like her person.

For the first time since she was seventeen she hadn't felt alone. She had people who needed her, and people who cared for her, and this sense of belonging had made her feel… wonderful.

So no, she couldn't blame Billy for making her feel so much. There was no blame here. She'd wanted every minute with him she could have. It had actually been selfish on her part because she'd relished, cherished feeling good. She'd loved feeling happy. She hadn't even known it was possible to feel this way, not with someone else, not in her own skin. These past few weeks she had just loved Billy and Beck, and she'd come to love herself.

She loved herself for maybe the first time ever.

It had been a revelation to realize she didn't need big things, she didn't need multiple college degrees, didn't need others to be impressed by her, either. What she needed was to feel like she belonged somewhere, and she had belonged here, even if briefly.

The idea that she had to go now was beyond devastating. But obviously she couldn't stay. Billy had made it clear that it was time for her to move on. Her heart went out to April and all the women Billy said goodbye to. She imagined him having the goodbye conversation countless times with countless women. *It's over, time to move on, it's been fun but we have to get on with our lives, alone.*

Erika was awake most of the night, sleeping in just patches, opening her eyes every so often to look at her phone. When it was four fifteen she gave up trying to sleep, and turned on her light and packed. She tore a page from a notebook and wrote Billy a goodbye, asking him not to contact her, and to just let her go. When she was ready, she'd reach out about visits with Beck, but it might be months, might be next year. All she asked of him was to respect her need for a complete break at this time.

***

WHEN ERIKA EMERGED from her room the next morning she was shocked to see Ellen in the kitchen.

"What are you doing here?" Erika asked.

Ellen faced her, expression neutral. "Billy texted last night and asked if I'd watch Beck today. He said you each had plans and he needed childcare."

Erika's heart fell. If Billy had arranged childcare, he'd expected changes today. He'd either expected her to leave, or he was going to ask her to go.

Erika glanced out the kitchen window. The sun was rising in the sky, painting the top of the mountains pink and gold. "Since you're here, I think I'll just slip out now," she said. "Before everyone's awake. I'm terrible with goodbyes."

Ellen looked confused. "You're leaving?"

Erika nodded. "I need to get back to Riverside. It's going to be a long drive." And then she went to her room, left the goodbye letter on her bed, and collected her suitcases, carrying them outside to the trunk of her car.

Erika was glad Beck still slept. She didn't know how she'd say goodbye to him without falling apart, and Beck didn't need drama swirling around him. Conversely, there was no point saying goodbye to Billy. What would she say to him anyway? And what would he say to her? She might as well save them an uncomfortable farewell where meaningless words would be exchanged.

In her car she buckled up, and reversed, before pulling out of the driveway. She drove down the road at a moderate speed until she hit the highway, and then once there, drove fast, the speed a relief.

Her heart burned, and her chest burned, and her eyes

burned. She was on fire, head to toe, and she drove as if she could escape the pain within her. She hurt and hurt and hurt, her entire past with all the abandonment and hollow goodbyes rising up to swamp her, reminding her just how easy it was for people to leave, to walk away. Her dad hadn't just left Mom, but he'd left her. Mom had disappeared into anger and her new church, where she could pretend she was loving and kind, as long as she didn't have to interact with her own daughter.

Even though she wanted to cry, she held the tears back. It was hard to breathe, hard to see, and it took her a moment to react when the car in front of her suddenly slammed on its brakes.

She slammed on her brakes, too, so hard that the back of the car fishtailed and she did a partial doughnut on the highway before coming to stop on the road's shoulder. Thank God the shoulder of the road was flat, and there had been room to skid to a stop. With the sound of screeching tires still ringing in her ears, she turned off the engine and rested her head on the steering wheel. She had to pull herself together. She couldn't tune out while driving. She'd get herself killed, or worse, hurt someone else.

Sitting in the car, the pain bubbled up again. She couldn't believe she was actually leaving Beck, for good this time.

She didn't want to walk away from him. Beck felt like hers… her baby, her son. She didn't feel like the cousin once removed anymore, she felt like Mom. Maybe because he had no other mom, or maybe because she'd given him all of her, but to leave a child she loved felt like a sin.

Love was awful. Love hurt. Love—

She lifted her head at the sound of a sharp rap on her window. Looking up she saw Billy standing there, handsome as ever, hair disheveled, jaw covered in stubble, a furious glint in his blue eyes.

It was the real him, a very raw him, not the charming polished cowboy that did appearances and signed cards at autograph sessions.

Her insides did a crazy flip and she rolled her window down, but then couldn't think of anything to say, and so she just stared up at him, shocked. Confused.

"You're just leaving without saying goodbye?" he demanded curtly, voice hard.

She blinked, eyes so gritty and dry. "I didn't think there was much for either of us to say."

"After all this time together, you don't think goodbye would have been nice? You don't think we needed some kind of closure?"

Closure made her throat swell, and her chest ache. "I got the closure last night," she whispered. "You made it clear I was no longer needed and so I'm moving on. I'm saving you from giving that speech you have to give to all your other girls—"

"You're not the others. You're not one of anyone else.

You weren't ever my buckle bunny. You were not a hookup. How could you even say that?"

"Because there's nothing for me here. There's nothing I can be—"

"No? Nothing for Beck? Did he matter so little to you?"

"He matters so much," she answered, her voice cracked with emotion. "He's like… mine. I've been with him for months. I have cared for him for months. I've woken up in the night to make sure he was okay for months. You think I want to leave him? You think I just want to play patty-cake and go?" She slammed her hands on the steering wheel. "But what am I to do, Billy? What are my options? How do we make this work? Because I can't hang around here and watch you with another woman. I don't want to look away every time your phone buzzes with a text from one of your girls. I don't want to dread the next rodeo because you have someone special in that town. I can't do that. I can't take care of Beck and look the other way while you are playing the field. I know I'm not yours, and I know we don't have a relationship, but I can't pretend that it doesn't tear me apart that you have someone else."

Erika reached up and wiped away the tears before they could fall. Her nose was congested. She could hardly breathe. She was saying too much, she was revealing too much, but she couldn't stop herself now. "I have real feelings for you, Billy. I fell for you, way too hard. It wasn't the plan. God knows it wasn't the plan. But it happened and I don't need you giving me your farewell speech that you've given to countless other women. It would kill me. Let me leave with some dignity. Let me go while I still have some self-respect."

"No," he said. "I'm not letting you go. And I don't give a damn for your self-respect, not when I think your judgment is clouded. If I thought it was the best thing for you to leave, I'd let you leave, but it's not the best thing for you, and it's not the best thing for me. We're good together, really good together, and I was going to say all of this to you today, before you snuck out of the house, and flew down the road like a crazed banshee."

"I didn't sneak anywhere. I left you a note—"

"I saw the note. It was ridiculous. You're being ridiculous—"

"Me? The man who won't commit to anyone or anything, the one who needs a different woman in every town—"

"Before you, yes. Before you, I did a lot of dumb things, but that was before you. Now there is you, and you change everything. *Everything.*"

"What are you saying?"

"Because of you, there will never be anyone else for me, not now. There is only you. You, Erika Baylor. You're mine. You belong with me. We're meant to be together. You, Beck, me. And if we're lucky, babies we make together."

He reached inside her car, unlocked the door, and opened it so that he could unbuckle her seat belt and pull her out onto her feet. "I'm not perfect, I'm far from perfect, but, sweetheart, I think I am perfect for you. And I don't say that arrogantly, I say it from the heart. Because I like you, I like you so much I can't think of one thing I don't like about you. I never get tired of your company. All I want to do is look up and see you. I love your voice. I love the way you sing as you cook or wash up—"

"I have a terrible voice. I can't carry a tune," she protested, leaning against him because her legs had no strength. Fortunately, he was warm and strong.

"I know, and I love that about you, because you sing anyway." He brushed a long tendril from her damp cheek, his fingertips infinitely gentle. "I love the way you frown at your computer when you're concentrating. I love the way you ask me to turn the TV down when it's too loud—"

"I try to be polite."

"I know, and you are. Excruciatingly polite." His thumb stroked her cheek, a slow comforting caress. "I love that you read to Beck even though he has no idea what you're saying—"

"But he does. He's really smart."

The corner of Billy's mouth lifted. "I love that you talk to him like he's a grown-up, and how he hangs onto every word you say."

"Because he's smart," she said, snuggling into his chest.

Billy laughed softly. "I love that you love him, because I know you do." His smile faded, his blue gaze growing somber. "You can't leave us, babe. You can't leave the people who need you, and we need you, Beck and me. We're your family. You're our family. We belong together."

He was saying so many lovely words, and saying things that made her feel better, but she was still afraid. Still worried. "But if there wasn't Beck, we wouldn't be together. You wouldn't want me, or need me—"

"Not true. You're not like anyone else I've ever known. You're stronger, and braver, and more loyal and more loving—you remind me of a Wyatt. You're my people. My person. I've been looking all my life for you." He kissed her then, a slow, persuasive kiss that seemed to kiss away her hurt. "Beck was just the one that brought us together, but we're meant to be together. Destined."

Destined. She liked the sound of that, and blinking, she looked up into his face, her gaze meeting his and holding. "You've turned my life inside out. It will break my heart for you to go, but—"

"I'm not going anywhere. I've chased you down because I can't lose you. I don't want you to leave. I don't know how to say fancy words, Erika. I'm not good with romance. But I sure as hell don't want to live life without you, not ever."

"You like me better than the others?"

He stared deep into her eyes, baffled. "I love you. I want to marry you and spend the rest of my life with you. So yes, I like you better than the others. I like you best of all. You're my girl. My one and only. I swear to you."

"Does that mean we have a relationship?"

He laughed, a soft husky laugh. "We better. I'm planning on marrying you very soon."

She rose up on tiptoe and kissed him, her arms wrapping around his neck. "Say that again."

"You're my girl."

"No, the other part."

"My one and only."

"No, the part about us having a relationship."

"You said that, not me."

She tipped her head back and looked up into his blue eyes. "But we do, right?"

"Yes."

"Say that to me."

"We have a relationship. We're in a relationship. It's an official relationship."

Erika grinned. "That sounds nice."

"What about the marrying soon part?"

"Oh, that was nice, too." She leaned in and kissed him. "Was that a proposal?" she asked against his mouth.

"No, I'm just stating my intentions. You'll know when I propose to you. You won't have to ask." He hesitated. "But just to be clear, you love me?"

"I love you more than anything. I love you until the end of time." She hesitated. "But I want time with you. I want you around for a very long time. Please don't go back on the circuit just yet. Please give yourself more time to heal. I couldn't bear it if anything happened to you again, not so soon—"

"I won't go back until next year. We'll spend the next seven months together, doing things together, enjoying being a family."

Her heart did a double beat. "Do you really mean that?"

"I do. But I have something to ask of you."

"What's that?"

"Finish your dissertation. Get it done. You'll feel so much better when it's completed, and you're free."

"I don't want to miss out on life—"

"You won't. Beck and I will be here every single day, supporting you, believing in you. Just pretend we're your dedicated fans in the stands cheering you on."

She leaned in for another kiss. "I like the sound of that. Erika Baylor, cowgirl."

"Erika Baylor Wyatt, my cowgirl."

Epilogue

B**ILLY WAS AS** good as his word.

He did not return to the professional rodeo circuit that year, taking the rest of the summer and fall off to heal and spend time with his son and Erika, while Erika returned to her studies, and devoted the summer to finishing her dissertation.

They spent most of their time at his cabin—their cabin—although every four weeks or so they made the drive to Paradise Valley to spend a few days with his family. Sam and Tommy were still doing well on the circuit and weren't home often, but Billy was always glad to see Granddad, Mom, Joe and Sophie.

Sophie and Joe's baby, Elijah Michael Wyatt, arrived early June, so there were two baby boy Wyatts for the next generation. It was just a matter of time before Beck and Elijah would become best friends. As it was, Beck was happy taking Elijah's toys from him, one after the other.

Erika had to defend her dissertation in mid-November. She passed, and was awarded her PhD. Beck's first birthday fell on Thanksgiving weekend just a week later, and all the

Wyatts made a point of returning to the Diamond W Ranch to celebrate Beck's birthday properly. There was a cake, balloons, streamers. Erika was delighted by Beck's joy, pounding on his tray of the old wooden highchair, screeching as he reached for a balloon. He was still, in her mind, the smartest baby ever and she couldn't believe how far they'd all come in the past nine months. It was while she was cutting Beck's birthday cake she hit something hard and she pulled out the knife, and looked at the cake worriedly. "I just hit something hard," she said. "Something is in the cake."

"Oh no," Sophie said. "How is that possible? I made the cake myself."

"That's not totally true," Joe said. "You had Billy's help. Didn't he help scrape the bowl?"

Sophie made a face. "More like licked the batter from the beaters," she said. She turned and glared at Billy. "I hope you didn't do anything to my cake."

Billy just shrugged. "I don't know what you're talking about. I just scraped the batter into the pans and put the pans in the oven like you said."

Erika sliced the next piece and put it on a dessert plate. And there in the middle of the second layer of the cake was something that should not be there, something silver, and— she used her fingers to pull it from the cake—and a diamond. A ring. A huge diamond ring.

"I think that's your slice," Billy said helpfully. "At least it should be now that you've gone and put your fingers all in it."

"My slice?" Erika repeated. "But there's a ring—" And then she looked at Billy and saw his smile, and sat down hard onto the edge of her dining chair. "Is this a joke?" Her voice quivered and she carefully wiped some of the cake and frosting from the huge marquis-cut diamond.

"No, not a joke." Billy stepped around the high chair and knelt at Erika's side. "Erika Baylor, will you do me the honor, the very great honor, of being my wife?" And Billy, being Billy, took the ring with the remnants of cake and icing and slid it on her finger even as she stared at him in shock.

"You're not kidding." Her eyes locked with his. Her heart pounded. She curled her fingers around his hand suddenly feeling faint, and she never felt faint. "This is the proposal."

He rose and pulled her to her feet. "This is the proposal." He kissed her in front of everyone. "Will you marry me?"

She blinked back tears, her eyes burning hot and salty, her throat aching with emotion. "I can't believe this is happening."

"So is that a yes?" he said in a mock whisper.

She laughed against his chest, her face buried against his shirt. He was so warm, he smelled so good. He felt, as always, just like home. "That's a yes, Billy Wyatt."

Billy hugged her closer, even as he looked to his family. "The girl said yes."

His family cheered, and Beck, having no idea about what was really going on, cheered too, hitting the wooden tray with all his might.

Billy kissed Erika again, sealing the deal. "Let's get married soon. I want you to be my wife before the end of the year."

She drew back to look up into his face, and his gorgeous blue eyes. "Are you thinking a Christmas wedding?"

"I'm just thinking soon; I'll let you decide the rest."

"Then a small Christmas wedding it is. Just family." She looked around the dining room, smiling at everyone. "Just all of you."

Want more? Check out Cade and Merri's romance in
Montana Cowboy Miracle!

Join Tule Publishing's newsletter for more great reads and weekly deals!

The Wyatt Brothers of Montana Series

Book 1: *Montana Cowboy Romance*

Book 2: *Montana Cowboy Christmas*

Book 3: *Montana Cowboy Daddy*

Book 4: *Montana Cowboy Miracle*

MORE BY JANE PORTER

Love on Chance Avenue series

Book 1: *Take Me, Cowboy*
Winner of the RITA® Award for Best Romance Novella

Book 2: *Miracle on Chance Avenue*

Book 3: *Take a Chance on Me*

Book 4: *Not Christmas Without You*

The Taming of the Sheenans series

The Sheenans are six powerful wealthy brothers from Marietta, Montana. They are big, tough, rugged men, and as different as the Montana landscape.

Christmas at Copper Mountain
Book 1: Brock Sheenan's story

Tycoon's Kiss
Book 2: Troy Sheenan's story

The Kidnapped Christmas Bride
Book 3: Trey Sheenan's story

Taming of the Bachelor
Book 4: Dillion Sheenan's story

A Christmas Miracle for Daisy
Book 5: Cormac Sheenan's story

The Lost Sheenan's Bride
Book 6: Shane Sheenan's story

ABOUT THE AUTHOR

New York Times and USA Today bestselling author of over fifty five romances and women's fiction titles, **Jane Porter** has been a finalist for the prestigious RITA award five times and won in 2014 for Best Novella with her story, Take Me, Cowboy, from Tule Publishing. Today, Jane has over 12 million copies in print, including her wildly successful, Flirting With Forty, picked by Redbook as its Red Hot Summer Read, and reprinted six times in seven weeks before being made into a Lifetime movie starring Heather Locklear. A mother of three sons, Jane holds an MA in Writing from the University of San Francisco and makes her home in sunny San Clemente, CA with her surfer husband and two dogs.

Thank you for reading

Montana Cowboy Daddy

If you enjoyed this book, you can find more from all our great authors at TulePublishing.com, or from your favorite online retailer.